How could she pray when she didn't know if God would hear?

Ann did not know how much time passed. The Prentisses drifted away at dusk, and it was fully dark when she heard the minister's steps on the deck. He came to them, saying nothing, and embraced William. He picked Jonathan up and held the boy, murmuring to him, then turned to Ann, still holding her brother. She could not see Caleb's face, but the cheek he touched to hers was damp—from his tears or the others', she could not tell.

"It is over," he said softly, and Ann felt the deck slipping away under her feet, and a long fall into darkness.

LOVE'S GENTLE JOURNEY

Kay Cornelius

Serenade/Saga
BOOKS
of the Zondervan Publishing House
Grand Rapids, Michigan

A Note From the Author:
I love to hear from my readers! You may correspond with me by writing:

> Kay Cornelius
> 1415 Lake Drive, S.E.
> Grand Rapids, MI 49506

LOVE'S GENTLE JOURNEY
Copyright © 1985 by The Zondervan Corporation
Grand Rapids, Michigan

Serenade/Saga is an imprint of Zondervan Publishing House,
1415 Lake Drive, S.E., Grand Rapids, Michigan 49506.

ISBN 0-310-47002-1

*Edited by Nancye Willis
and Anne Severance
Designed by Kim Koning*

Printed in the United States of America

85 86 87 88 89 90 91 / 10 9 8 7 6 5 4 3 2 1

To God be the glory

CHAPTER 1

ANN STOOD ON THE DECK of the *Derry Crown* and looked about her, overwhelmed by the mélange of sights, sounds, and smells aboard the square-rigged sailing vessel, and compelled to let its many new sensations wash over her without making any attempt to sort them all out. In the month since her father's decision to leave Ireland, she had often wondered what this day would be like. Now it was here, and nothing was as she had imagined.

"Come, lass, help your mother below," said William McKay as he set down the last bundle of their small store of worldly goods.

Ann helped her mother rise from the trunk where she had been sitting. The winter of 1739-40, just past, had been harsh, and she was alarmed that Sarah's cough still lingered.

Despite the older woman's pallor and the dark shadows under her eyes, the resemblance between them was striking. Both women were blessed with gentle features and great dark eyes; though, at seventeen, Ann's figure was still girlish and only hinted of the beauty she would become. Sarah McKay, just over twice her daughter's age, moved slowly, as if trying to conserve her meager energy.

Suddenly she stopped and looked anxiously about the deck. "Where is Jonathan?"

"Over there," her husband replied, nodding toward the aft rigging where the seven-year-old's curly head was bent in earnest conversation with one of the sailors. "There's much for the lad to see."

"Look to him, William. I believe I'll rest a bit before we sail."

Leaning heavily on Ann's arm, Sarah moved toward the narrow passageway leading to the cramped quarters that would be their home for the next two months. The McKays had been given a set of double bunks near the foot of the stairs, though the close confinement did not even allow one to sit on the lower bunks. Indeed, only curtains of some coarse fabric separated them from the next family's allotted space.

Ann eased her mother onto the bottom bunk and spread her shawl over her. "I'll go help Father with our things if there's naught else I can do for ye now," she said.

"No, don't go just yet, daughter. I would have a word with ye. Pull up that stool yonder and sit down."

Ann did as her mother asked, taking the frail hand the woman extended to her. "I can see that ye are grieving over this journey," Sarah began, and although Ann shook her head in denial, her eyes filled with tears.

"Our life at Coleraine was all I ever knew. I just feel . . . " She paused, not knowing how to describe her turmoil since her father's decision to emigrate to the American plantation country.

Like most of their neighbors, the McKays were Scots, and although the family had lived in Ireland for three generations, they clung to their Scottish ways.

8

From the porridge they ate in the morning to the Border ballads they sang each evening, the Scots, who had been brought from their lowland homes to curb the papist influence of the native Irish, had retained their own ways. Living in a land where the dispossessed Irish despised them, and their absentee English landlords exacted a heavy toll for the right to use their land, had not been easy, but they had always made the best of their situation.

Therefore, it was a surprise to learn that William McKay was ready to cast his lot, and that of his family, with the others leaving the green-gold hills of Ulster for the colonies in the new world. A surprise—and a bitter disappointment.

"Take heart, daughter," Sarah encouraged softly, squeezing Ann's hand. "'Twas hard for me to leave Scotland when I wed your father. 'Twas hard to leave our little ones who sleep in the churchyard. But we are together in this. Your father had no choice, for a man has to make a living for his family. It is best for us to accept what must be."

Accept it she must, but she would miss the bony cow she milked twice a day, the soft, fluffy fleeces of the spring lambs, and the downy yellow chicks she raised and sold at the market. Ann had tried to imagine what America was like, but she could not, any more than she was able to picture the Scots town where her mother had been born and to which she had always longed to return. Ann had been to Coleraine, and the village of Downready, and last year she had bought some bright hair ribbons at the Cleary Fair, but she had never been to Londonderry, or ridden in a carriage, or sat in a boat. And of all these unfamiliar things, Ann was afraid. She listened as her father led their family prayer time by thanking God for the way they had been shown and asking Him to grant them a safe passage, and she was not comforted.

"I did not mean to complain," Ann said, her eyes downcast.

"Ye must have faith, Ann, and trust that God is working in all of it."

Ann was silent, feeling the hot tears squeeze through her closed lids. To her, the God of the church had always seemed a remote, silent judge. The small kirk where Reverend Duffie preached the Calvinist creed had never comforted her. She could not follow the long sermons, and the backless benches that served as pews grew harder and harder. Out of doors, where the storm clouds moved with awful majesty, and the covenant of the rainbow arched over the Ulster hills, Ann could feel a peace in the wonder of God's creation. But He had never seemed a guiding Presence in her life as He obviously was in her mother's. Even William, though he attended Sabbath services and dutifully led their daily prayers, was not as devout as his wife.

"I would like to believe that God is guiding us," she said in a weak voice.

Sarah sighed. "Ye will need more than your own strength to help Jonathan and your father when I am gone."

"Hush, Mother!" cried Ann in alarm.

"Listen to me now, child. I want ye to have my Bible. Keep it with your things."

"But—"

"Read it, child, and keep its words in your heart. 'Lean not unto thine own understanding,' the Scriptures tell us. Will ye promise to do that?"

"Yes," Ann said faintly.

"Now ye should go back to your father, dear. This time together has done me good. And, Ann," Sarah added, touching her daughter's face tenderly, "ye are not to worry him. Do ye understand that?"

Ann nodded, too near tears to speak. Her father must know, she thought, and even Jonathan could see that their mother had not recovered her health, indeed, was growing weaker by the day. Ann could only do as she was instructed . . . and hope.

The brightness of the morning sun, in sharp contrast to the dimness below, caused Ann to blink as she climbed to the upper deck. If anything, the confusion here had increased, she thought. The docks teemed with sailors, passengers, agents, and hawkers, all moving amidst general noise and confusion. Swarthy sailors came and went, hauling aboard great casks and wooden crates. Occasionally some of them would glance her way, exchange a comment in some unknown tongue, then laugh uproariously. Ann felt uncomfortable and ducked into a more secluded passageway where she could view the happenings unseen.

She tried not to stare at the women who thronged around the sailors, hanging onto their arms and even touching their faces. Their bodices were cut astonishingly low, and their lips and cheeks were unnaturally red. Ann had heard rouged women spoken of in whispers, but she had never before actually seen any. She glanced at Jonathan, but he was absorbed in watching a sailor with a beautifully-colored yellow and blue bird perched on his shoulder.

Here came other seamen and passengers up the gangplank, carrying sacks of provisions and barrels of grog and water. A few live animals were being prodded aboard, bawling and mooing their protest. Ann felt a momentary stab of sympathy. The poor things understood even less than she their sudden change of circumstance. Looking about for a glimpse of her father, she spied the bright red head of Isabel Prentiss.

"Hello, Ann!" the girl called, waving her hand. "I was wondering if ye had come aboard yet."

The Prentiss family had arrived in Londonderry about the same time as the McKays, and with the same intentions. Although Isabel was just past sixteen, she already had the full figure of a woman. Today, dressed in a frock of vivid blue, she looked

11

even older than her years, and Ann felt dowdy by comparison in her own drab homespun. Despite the differences in age and appearance, however, they had become friends, and Ann felt her heart lift a bit at the greeting.

"Oh, Isabel! Yes, we've been here for several hours now. My mother needed time to settle in before the crowds gathered."

"Have ye ever seen the likes of so many men!" Isabel cried, her eyes bright. "Why, there are more fine-lookin' young chaps in one place than ever set foot in Coleraine . . . or Londonderry, either, I'd vow. Mayhap this voyage won't be so bad, after all. A girl ought to be able to find a husband without half tryin'!"

"Most of the men I have seen are sailors, and look to be a rough lot," Ann observed.

"Yes, but there are lots of single men here, on their way to America, maybe even some rich ones wanting to invest in the colonies."

Ann glanced at Isabel, wondering if she had intended to make a joke, but the girl seemed quite serious. "Ye want a rich husband, then?"

"Why not? I'd like to have nice things and not be scolded if I spent a ha'penny now and again. How about ye, Ann? What sort of husband do ye seek?"

"I have not given it much thought," Ann said, half-truthfully.

"Well, ye ought to think about it," Isabel said firmly, with a characteristic toss of her red head. "If ye don't mind, ye'll likely wind up wedded wi' a poor crofter, and never have two coins to rub together. Look what's coming now!" cried Isabel, nodding toward the gangplank. Ann turned to see a party of men being escorted aboard ship. "Do ye suppose those are the prisoners being transported?"

It had been rumored that a number of convicts would be sailing with them, some of whom had asked to be sent to the colonies instead of remaining in Irish prisons. Others had been given no choice in the matter. There were at least a dozen of them, carefully guarded by red-coated soldiers carrying muskets.

"They aren't in chains," observed Ann, "but it appears that those soldiers are making certain they are safely aboard."

"They don't look like such a bad lot, do they?" Isabel mused, taking a closer look.

Most of the men were young and poorly garbed, but not any more so than most of the passengers.

"'Tis a shame. My father says many men who are transported come from debtors' prison . . . that their only crime is poverty." Ann shuddered, wondering if her father might have shared their fate.

The soldiers, having turned over their charges to a burly seaman with a look of authority, disembarked and stood on the dock at attention, evidently awaiting the launching of the ship.

When Ann looked back to the deck, a man was speaking to her brother Jonathan. Plainly but neatly dressed, he was smiling at something Jonathan was saying.

"Should your brother be talking to a convict?" asked Isabel.

"Mother would be much displeased, I'm sure," Ann agreed. "But here comes my father. He'll attend to it."

As William started toward them, the man tousled Jonathan's hair and moved on toward the passageway leading to the deck where the sailors and single men were quartered. Unlike the others who carried cloth or canvas duffel bags, he was holding a large wooden box. Ann wondered what it might contain.

"Oh, let's listen to the captain, Ann. He's about to speak." Isabel interrupted Ann's thoughts and moved nearer the upper deck, where the captain had taken a position near the wheel and was calling the noisy crowd to attention.

13

"Hear ye! Hear ye! I wish to see the head of every household, the eldest males traveling with families, and all other single men here on the wheel deck. We sail with the tide to Cork. There we'll pick up two other vessels to form a convoy. Then we're bound for the port of Philadelphia. May the good Lord grant His mercy on our voyage."

A few scattered "Amens" were heard as the men pressed toward the designated meeting place. Jonathan and Sarah, who had left her bunk, were standing by Ann. She tried to count the men as they passed by, but soon gave up. Of the women and children who were left on the lower deck, there seemed to be around thirty, more than she had expected could be comfortably accommodated on a vessel as small as the *Derry Crown*.

"I wonder what the captain is saying," said Isabel.

"He might be telling them about *pirates*," Jonathan suggested, so solemnly that the girls laughed.

"You and your pirates!" Ann exclaimed fondly. "Such notions you have! And I suppose ye'll be disappointed if we don't see any the whole voyage, won't ye?"

"Ye jest, Mistress Ann, but I heard the sailors talking of it," young Samuel Prentiss put in. "They said pirates like the English ships best, but will take a merchant ship like ours if it suits their fancy."

Mistress Prentiss joined them in time to hear her son's statement and nodded. "'Tis true, what the lad says. I heard the captain say we are meeting the other ships at Cork because there's some safety in numbers."

"I know what a pirate ship looks like," Jonathan volunteered. "She flies the Jolly Roger flag, with a cannon on every deck."

"Aye, and we have a cannon, too. Did ye notice?" asked Mistress Prentiss.

"It looks like a toy," shrugged Isabel. "I doubt it has ever been fired."

"And let us all pray that it need never be," Sarah said quietly.

"The captain must be through instructing the men, for here comes Father now." Ann was glad for the diversion. The conversation seemed to be taking a morbid turn, and her mother needed no further worries.

"Well, at last we are to get underway," he said with a cheerful air. "With fair winds and God's grace, we should make Philadelpia in eight or nine weeks."

Noting how pale and drawn Sarah looked, Ann felt that nine weeks would be quite a long time, but she kept silent, fearing to make bad matters worse. Isabel, on the other hand, was not so cautious.

"Well I, for one, don't know how we shall endure it. But I suppose the sooner we begin, the sooner we arrive."

They watched as the ropes securing the vessel to the dock were released. The anchor was raised, and the rigging came alive with clambering sailors, maneuvering the sails to catch the freshening wind. A few people on the dock waved and shouted farewells to relatives aboard ship.

Keenly aware that she might never again see her native country, Ann watched the green hills slip from sight. Her vision blurred, but she was determined not to cry.

"Look, Jonathan, the seagulls are following us," she called to her brother.

Wild and free, they soared above the billowing sails. And she watched them, wondering what it must be like to live untethered to the earth. Then the gulls, too, returned to shore and Ann resigned herself to the brave ship that plowed on, through the trackless ocean that stretched forever ahead.

CHAPTER 2

LIFE AT SEA, AT FIRST NOVEL and exciting, quickly settled into a routine. As planned, the *Derry Crown* met two other ships, the *Star* and *Regent*, at Cork, and the sight of their white sails moving along on either side was vastly reassuring.

The passengers soon found that the agent had exaggerated the vessel's virtues and neglected to mention its faults. The food rations, while adequate for sustenance, often left them unsatisfied. The passengers soon learned that it was best not to expend energy unnecessarily.

After a poor start of sleepless nights, the McKays finally adjusted themselves to the unaccustomed motion of the ship and to their cramped quarters. William often slept upon deck, and Sarah was allowed the most convenient bunk, the middle one, to herself. When William slept below, Ann and Jonathan shared the bottom bunk.

The boy seemed to enjoy everything about the voyage. Despite his father's warnings to be careful, Jonathan wandered freely about the ship, talking to everyone who would listen and asking endless questions.

The single men, including the group being transported, were quartered with the sailors, one level below the family deck. They generally used the port side of the upper deck, although no restrictions had been placed on any of the passengers.

Ann and Isabel found a sheltered spot on the starboard side of the deck, where they sometimes watched the single men as they took the air. Although Isabel had dismissed them as unlikely marriage prospects, some of the men were young and attractive.

A few days into the voyage, the man who had spoken to Jonathan the day they boarded nodded to them. Much younger than her father, he appeared to be perhaps a dozen years her senior. With his expressive brown eyes and broad brow, he was what many would call handsome, yet his air seemed unusually grave. The man was holding a book, and, as they watched, he leaned against a bulwark and began to read.

"I wonder what he did to be transported," Isabel said. "He looks like a real gentleman, compared to the others."

"Oh, he isn't one of them," Jonathan volunteered. "I think he's a schoolmaster, because he asked me if I thought Father might allow him to give us lessons."

"A schoolmaster!" Isabel exclaimed. "Perhaps he'll take the boys in hand, then!"

"Aye, the children on board need something to fill their time and keep them from mischief," agreed Ann.

"I'll go ask him about it," said Jonathan, and was gone before Ann could open her mouth in protest.

When Jonathan returned, he was wriggling with excitement. "I am to tell Father that Mr. Craighead is willing to teach any who wish it," he said importantly.

At his son's urging, William conferred with the schoolmaster that morning.

17

"He seems to be a good sort," William told Sarah later as the family gathered for prayer. Subject to the captain's approval, Caleb Craighead would commence teaching the very next day. "Perhaps Jonathan will learn some of his letters by the time we reach Philadelphia."

"I know some of them already," Jonathan boasted, "and I know lots of numbers and things."

"Ye still have much to learn," Sarah smiled fondly. "Yes, William, it is good for the children to be occupied in a useful manner. Surely the captain can have no objections."

Captain Murdock readily agreed to the proposal, providing Mr. Craighead keep the younger children out of the sailors' way. The next day six boys and four girls, ranging in age from seven to fourteen, assembled on the aft deck for their first session.

Ann and Isabel stationed themselves nearby, pretending to be fully absorbed with their knitting, but sharply aware of all that was going on around them. Mr. Craighead's black box, which had caught Ann's attention as he came on board, yielded a variety of interesting materials. In addition to textbooks of the kind used in the school Reverend Duffie kept in Coleraine, he had a Bible, a Psalter, and the Westminster catechism, which most of the older children had already learned to recite from memory.

Mr. Craighead also had a shallow sandbox, in which the young ones practiced shaping their letters, using their forefingers. The sand could be smoothed again with a shake of the box, and even the older children, using feathered quills, used it to practice their handwriting. Sometimes Mr. Craighead set sums for his students, making the numbers in the sand and letting them take turns ciphering out the answers.

The only reader was the Bible, and often Mr. Craighead read it to them himself, in a firm, resonant voice that, with its Scots burr, was quite pleasant to

18

hear. Ann and Isabel, though several years older than the pupils, listened along with them, glad for the diversion.

The school had been underway for some two weeks when the fair weather finally broke, and squalls of wind-driven rain kept the passengers below. Mr. Craighead tried holding lessons in the cramped family dining area, but the light was poor, and as the storm grew more intense, the motion of the ship made reading impossible.

"I had thought a spring passage would be calmer than fall or winter," William commented on the second day of their confinement.

For the first time, the movement of the ship made Ann feel ill, and she stayed in her bunk, grasping its sides as the vessel tossed and pitched. How long could the groaning timbers of the ship stand such buffeting without splitting asunder?

Twice daily a sailor came down to the family deck, carrying a bucket of water and another filled with the thin gruel the captain had ordered as their storm fare, but few of the passengers even attempted to partake of it. The sailor Jonathan called Ian brought them some hardtack on the third day of the storm, and at his urging they each broke off a piece and chewed it gingerly. "We should be out o' this blow by dawn," he assured them. "The wind has shifted direction, and the clouds are breakin' up."

Just before sunrise the next morning Ann, feeling weak and lightheaded from the combined effects of the lack of food and the rankness of their quarters, stumbled up the stairs to the deck and leaned weakly against the rail, breathing in the fresh air. Some half-dozen others had come up onto deck by the time the sun appeared, and Ann saw that the schoolmaster was among them.

"Good morning, Mistress McKay," he greeted,

19

walking over to stand beside her. "How has your family withstood the storm?"

Ann looked up at Caleb Craighead, suddenly overcome with shyness. In all her years, Ann had never held a conversation with a man alone. His gray eyes were quietly reassuring, and Ann yearned again for an appearance that matched her years and for the facility to converse with him as easily as he was speaking to her. It seemed a very long time before she managed to say anything.

"We have all survived, thank ye," she finally said, "but for a time I feared I would not." Then, afraid her remark had been too personal, she blushed.

Apparently Mr. Craighead did not notice her discomfort, for he continued. "The captain says we must expect at least one more spell of bad weather before we make port."

"Can the ship withstand another storm?" Ann asked, alarmed at the thought of repeating their recent experience.

"It has done so many times before," he assured her. "Tell your brother and my other pupils that lessons will resume today for all who are able to come."

"Jonathan was the least affected of us all," Ann said. "He will be happy to be occupied again."

"And I shall be glad, as well. I am unaccustomed to idleness." Mr. Craighead touched a hand to his forehead in a gesture of farewell, wished Ann a good day, and walked away.

As Ann watched him go, her head was still light, but a strange warmth filled her heart. *He thinks of me as a child*, she mused, knowing full well that Isabel would have known just what to say—and how. As she went below, Ann found herself hoping that he would seek her out again.

Jonathan was taking breakfast when Ann returned to their quarters, and William was attempting to persuade Sarah to eat a bowl of gruel.

"I can't swallow a drop," she protested, but at her husband's encouragement, she managed a few spoonfuls.

"The sun is out, and it promises to be a beautiful day," Ann told her mother. "Let us help ye up on deck. Ye'll feel better for having some fresh air."

"But she must not be chilled," William warned. "Wait until the sun is higher, and the air warms."

By then, the deck was crowded with all the passengers who were able to walk. Most of Caleb Craighead's pupils were back, and he entertained them with stories of various biblical storms, while Sarah and Ann sat nearby, listening along with the children.

When he finished and had set the children to various tasks, Sarah spoke to him. "Mr. Craighead, the way ye tell those stories puts me in mind of a pastor I knew in Scotland in the old days. Have ye ever felt a call to the ministry, by any chance?"

Ann had never known a minister who looked—or sounded—like Mr. Craighead, and she was surprised when he nodded.

"I have, ma'am. In fact, after serving as a schoolmaster for some years, I have only recently been ordained to the ministry. It is my intention to preach in America, as God leads me."

"Ah," said Sarah. "Then perhaps ye can lead us in worship of a Sabbath on this ship?"

"If Captain Murdock has no objections, and will tell us when the Lord's Day is," he smiled. "I fear that I may have lost a day during the storm."

"Please ask him," Sarah urged. "We all need to hear the Word proclaimed, no matter where we may be."

"I do hope Mr. Craighead will not be long-winded," Isabel said as she and Ann waited for him to begin the first service two days later. "Our pastor

21

always spoke at least two hours, and never said anything I could remember two minutes later.''

''Perhaps his preaching will be as interesting as his teaching,'' Ann replied.

''Well, in any case we canna leave if we don't like it. 'Twould be a long swim back to Ireland,'' Isabel proclaimed, tossing her head and smiling. Then she took a quick look about to see if any of the men were noticing.

Caleb Craighead, minister, looked no different to Ann from Caleb Craighead, schoolmaster, except for the white linen shirt replacing his usual brown one. Either he lacked a black ecclesiastical suit, or had chosen not to wear it.

Standing on the captain's deck, Caleb looked out over his makeshift congregation. Nearly all of the passengers had gathered for the service, including most of the men who were being transported, and even a few of the sailors. His voice was firm and clear as he led in a long prayer, and then asked one of the men to line out a hymn from the Psalter. Another read from the Scriptures, then Caleb Craighead began his sermon. All listened with attention as he began to talk in quiet, almost conversational tones, of God's grace and mercy, of His ability to protect them if they trusted Him utterly.

Reverend Duffie had never preached with such force or quiet conviction, and as Ann listened, she thought about what this unlikely young minister was saying. Did God really care about them, she wondered? Did He know, right now, this instant, that this band of people was here, on this tiny ship in the midst of a vast ocean? There could be no doubt that Caleb earnestly believed that God was with them, but it was almost too much for Ann to accept.

''Well, that didn't take too long,'' Isabel said after the benediction. ''Do ye think Captain Murdock'd loan us his spyglass? I want to see if the other ships are still with us.''

"I am sure they are," Ann said, turning away. She did not want Isabel to see her face; she was not even sure what was written there herself, but whatever it was, she meant to keep it private. "I must see to Mother's bedding before she comes below," she added, and hastened away before Isabel could reply.

The next week continued mostly calm and fair, but there was often a chill in the air, and Sarah had begun to cough again, so she rarely ventured on deck. Ann spent much time with her mother, reading aloud Psalms and Scripture passages that Sarah knew from memory. Each day when his lessons were finished, Caleb Craighead came to sit at Sarah's bedside, and Ann looked forward to his visits, although he rarely spoke directly to her. Caleb spoke of his childhood in Scotland, not far from where Sarah was born, and of going up to the university at Edinburgh. Often a fit of coughing would seize Sarah, and although she turned her head away from them, Ann could see the crimson stains in the cloth her mother held to her lips, and her heart ached. It was apparent that Sarah was worsening daily.

"Father, is there naught we can do?" Ann asked one evening after Sarah had suffered a particularly violent spell of coughing. "I feel so helpless."

"Aye, lass," William agreed sadly. "There's no surgeon on board, and such physic as the captain has canna' heal, but only ease pain."

"She says she feels no pain, but her eyes tell a different tale. Perhaps ye could ask Captain Murdock for some laudanum."

William nodded and went in search of the captain, but when he returned with it, Sarah would not take the draught.

"Fetch Mr. Craighead," she asked. "I have need of his prayers tonight."

When Caleb Craighead arrived, prayer book in

hand, Sarah motioned to her family. "Leave us alone, now."

Ann bent down and kissed her mother's wasted cheek, her throat tight with the burden of unshed tears. Then she and William went up on deck, where Jonathan sat with the Prentisses.

"I saw Mr. Craighead go below," Jonathan said. "Is Mother worse, then?"

William did not reply, but patted his son's thin shoulder.

"I think we should offer prayer now, also," Mr. Prentiss suggested, and as they bowed their heads, he hesitantly began to recite the Lord's Prayer.

" 'Thy will be done,' " Ann repeated with them, but she did not understand what that really meant. How could she pray to a God whose will could take Sarah from a family that needed her sorely, when she had ever been His servant? Yet she could not help murmuring over and over, as if the mere repetition could help, "She must live, she can't die, she can't . . ."

Ann did not know how much time passed. The Prentisses drifted away at dusk, and it was fully dark when she heard the minister's steps on the deck. He came to them, saying nothing, and embraced William. He picked Jonathan up and held the boy, murmuring to him, then turned to Ann, still holding her brother. She could not see Caleb's face, but the cheek he touched to hers was damp—from his tears or the others', she could not tell.

"It is over," he said softly, and Ann felt the deck slipping away under her feet, and a long fall into darkness.

CHAPTER 3

WHEN ANN REGAINED HER SENSES she was lying in Isabel's bunk and Mary Prentiss was bending over her, pouring something down her throat. She began to choke and gasp.

"There, lass, 'twill do ye good. Swallow it down, now. That's a good girl."

"Where is Jonathan? And Father?" Ann asked, trying to rise. "I should be with them."

"Just lie still and rest. Everything has been seen to, and the others are asleep. Your father thought it best that ye bide wi' us for the night."

Ann looked at the drawn curtains around her family's bunks and saw that everyone else below seemed to be sleeping. "All right," she agreed. She wanted to ask what they had done with her mother's body, but she could not bring herself to speak of it.

Mrs. Prentiss patted Ann's hand and rose. "I'll just douse this candle, then," she said, "and crawl into the bunk above ye. Try to rest, and call me if ye have need of aught."

Ann murmured her thanks, but she did not think

she would sleep. The ship creaked and groaned as it usually did, the noise always more ominous during the long hours of the night. One of the babies fretted and was hushed. Mr. Simmons was snoring again, and Ann recalled with a pang how she and Sarah, both awakened by the noise the first night out, had stifled their laughter. Now Sarah would never hear anything, nor ever laugh again. Tears formed in Ann's eyes and rolled unchecked down her cheeks. Her mother was dead. She would never feel her tender touch, never again hear her soft voice. Ann had asked God to spare her, but her plea had not been heard.

"Why?" she asked, forming the word silently in the darkness. No answer came, and eventually, Ann fell into an exhausted slumber.

It was not yet quite dawn when Ann was brought up to the deck for her mother's funeral. Some of the women had laid Sarah out in her good black wool dress, and she looked as if sleeping on the deck of a ship at dawn were the most natural thing in the world. A small number of their company gathered around the trestle of boards in the center of the deck as the captain conducted the ceremony. He seemed to be accustomed to the role, seldom referring to the book he held. Ann barely heard Mr. Craighead's brief eulogy, though she caught his reference to Sarah as a woman whose children "rose up and called her blessed," a woman who loved and feared the Lord and walked ever in His ways.

Ann stood between her father and Jonathan, who stared straight ahead, his face expressionless. Her brother was strangely quiet, and, for his sake, she held his hand tightly and willed herself not to cry. William had aged ten years in the uncertain morning light, and he kept rubbing his eyes with the back of his hand, as if dust had blown into them.

The captain's voice droned on: "Let not your heart

be troubled: ye believe in God, believe also in me. In my father's house are many mansions: if it were not so, I would have told you. I go to prepare a place for you .... I am the resurrection and the life: he that believeth in me, though he were dead, yet shall he live: And whosoever liveth and believeth in me shall never die. . . .''

Ann heard the words, comfortless. A cool breeze sprang up, and she shivered. As the last prayer was said, the captain signaled two sailors, who covered Sarah's body and moved the catafalque to the rail.

"Unto thy depths do we commit the body of thy servant, Sarah McKay," the captain pronounced, and the boards were tilted, sending their burden into the sea. There was a faint splash, then silence. The sailors and the captain began going about their business, and the passengers who had ventured up on deck for the service began to scatter, most pausing briefly to express their sympathy.

"We thank ye," William said to Caleb Craighead when he joined them, "for your kind words."

"She was a fine woman," Caleb said, "and there can be no doubt that she is with the angels this morning."

"Can Mother see us, then?" asked Jonathan, gazing up at the brightening sky as if he half-expected to see her smiling down at him.

"Perhaps," the minister replied.

"But we shan't ever see her again?"

"No, lad, not on this earth. But come, ye are learning the catechism, and it tells us that 'the souls of believers are at their death made perfect in holiness, and do immediately pass into glory; and their bodies, being still united to Christ, do rest in their graves till the resurrection.' Do ye not recall those words?"

"Oh, I know all of that," Jonathan replied, then paused. "I just don't understand it yet."

"Aye, son," William said, half-smiling at the

remark, "and neither does any man. But come along now. We must go below."

With a nod in Caleb's direction, William steered Jonathan toward the stairs, but Ann made no move to follow them.

Caleb moved quietly to her side. "I was thinking that if there had been a surgeon on this vessel, my mother might still be alive. She should not have been taken," she said, her voice faltering.

"Some day, perhaps all ships will be required to carry surgeons," Caleb replied, "but until then, we must do the best we can. I have some stores that will be useful if a general fever breaks out—wormwood and rue to cleanse. As closely as we are confined, one fever can become an epidemic."

"Mother was ill before we left home, but we thought she was getting better. She did nothing to deserve her punishment," Ann said bitterly.

"Ah, lass, do not be angry. Ye have sustained a great loss, but ye must be strong for your family."

"But ye knew my mother. How could it be God's will to take her, kind and loving as she was?"

"I have not the answer to that. Ye know the catechism as well as I. If we knew the intent of God, He would na' be better than ourselves. Better to ask Him for strength, then to question what canna' be changed."

Tears came to Ann's eyes and she could not speak. Caleb was looking at her with such pity and concern that she felt ashamed.

"God will help ye, though I cannot," he said, taking her hand in his.

"There's no help for it," she said in a choked voice. "'Tis hard."

"I know, lass. Now go to your family, as your mother would want ye to do. Ye need one another now."

For several days Ann lay below deck on the bunk that had been her mother's deathbed and grieved, sometimes with tears, but often without. Fitfully she tried to pray, but her heart was not in the effort, and God seemed too far away and remote for any words of hers to have any effect. Maybe one day she could accept what had happened, but not now, not yet, she thought, and continued to keep to herself, until one afternoon when Jonathan was at his lessons and the others were taking the air on deck.

Ann forced herself to open the leather trunk that held her mother's things and sort the contents, knowing she must decide what to do with each item.

She could certainly use the winter cloak, the sturdy boots, and the petticoats. Sarah's dresses, like most of the family's clothing, were made of material she had spun herself: the linen, from flax they had grown; the wool, from sheep they had raised and shorn. The dresses were a bit long for Ann, but they would do; she would keep them all. The cloth from one could be recut for Jonathan, who would need warm clothing for the winter.

Ann set aside the garments and looked at the rest of her mother's small store of earthly goods. Ann had helped her pack these things —was it only a few short weeks past? Now, in this place, each was a sad reminder of the past. Her mother's only jewelry was a golden locket that had belonged to Ann's grandmother. It enclosed a ringlet of hair, and as Ann touched it, she realized that as a girl, Sarah's hair must have been very near the shade of Ann's own, a rich chestnut brown with shades of auburn.

Next Ann found the blue cashmere shawl William had given Sarah as a wedding gift, and which she had worn only on special occasions. A small parcel held some baby clothes, yellowed from age, that Ann had not known her mother had packed—hers, perhaps, or maybe even Sarah's, made with dainty stitches long ago.

Underneath it all, carefully wrapped in linen, lay the parts of Sarah's spinning wheel, along with her distaff and the carding combs. Their loom, too large and bulky to fit in their allotted luggage, had been sold, but Ann was glad they had brought the wheel. She had no idea if the packet of flax seeds William had brought would grow in their new home—wherever that might be—but if they could keep a few sheep, Ann knew she would be able to use the spinning wheel to help keep them warmly clothed.

"Oh, Ann, Mother was wondering if ye wanted us to do that," Isabel said, and Ann looked up to see her friend standing beside her, looking concerned.

"There's really naught to be done," Ann replied. "We sold most of what we had before we left home, including the coverlets and linens. Mother had not much that was her own."

"I know she set a great store by that book," Isabel said, nodding toward the Bible on the table.

"Aye, and she told me when we were still in port that I was to have it. She knew then that she'd not survive this voyage."

Isabel was silent for a moment, then remembered her errand. "Ann, I've been sent to bring ye up to the deck."

Ann pushed the trunk back under the lower bunk and stood. "Why? Is there trouble?"

Isabel lowered her voice, glancing back at a curtained area midway in the family passenger section. "The Fletcher boy is taken with a fever, and his baby sister is very ill with the same sickness. The captain told Father he doubted it was serious, but he said not to stay too close to them, all the same. I came to fetch ye to join the rest of us."

Ann followed Isabel up the stairs. On deck, she could not help glancing at the spot where Sarah's body had been let down into the sea. Where was it now, she wondered. Had it sunk to the bottom, or was it perhaps floating on top of the waves, like the drowned man Ann had once seen in Bailley Creek? She walked over to the rail and looked down at the foamy green water.

"Mistress McKay! Mistress Prentiss! Would you come over here, please?"

It was Caleb Craighead calling to them from the midst of a circle of children.

"What is it?" Isabel asked as the girls reached him.

"Would ye help with the lessons whilst I hear Mavis's catechism?"

Isabel looked uncomfortable. "I canna read to them," she said.

"That is fine—just trace letters for the little ones and watch to see if they can do them after you. Here, shake the sand smooth first. Mistress Ann, would ye read to the older ones?"

"I can try," she said. He handed her a well-thumbed copy of *The Pilgrim's Progress*, which she had heard him reading to the children earlier.

"Begin here," he directed, and moved to one side with Mavis McCarty.

Ann began to read the story of Christian, who trespassed on the grounds of Doubting Castle, where Giant Despair imprisoned Christian and his friend Hopeful. At last, after being beaten and tormented and threatened with death, Christian remembered a key called Promise in his bosom. Using the key, he and his friend managed to escape, whereupon Christian and Hopeful offered prayer for their deliverance. The children were intrigued with the adventure and begged for more when she ended the chapter. But Caleb was back now, and when she tried to return the book, he insisted she take it.

"Keep it for a time," he said. "Perhaps ye will be kind enough to read again to the children. Ye should read it yourself, if ye have never done so."

"I have not read it, and I thank ye."

"And thank ye both for the help. It was a pleasant change for the children."

"I can teach letters," Isabel said as they walked away, "but I could never read aloud as ye were doing. All those big words!"

"Mother made me read to her as soon as I half-learned how," Ann said. "Her eyes were weak, and she had trouble making out the words. We had no books, though, just Mother's Bible."

"The same with us," Isabel said. "Father says that's the only book fit to be read, anyway," she added.

"I think I'd like to read more of this book now, if you don't mind," Ann said.

"Oh, no, I don't mind. I'll just see what I can find in the spyglass."

But when Isabel had left, Ann sat with the book closed, and watched Caleb Craighead. And more than once, she caught him returning her glances.

In the next few days everyone seemed intent on keeping Ann and her family occupied. William joined in the men's endless talk about America to pass otherwise idle hours. Ian, one of the crew members, gave Jonathan a bit of wood and was teaching him to carve it into a ship. At his mother's urging, Samuel Prentiss began to spend more time with Jonathan after their lessons, and Ann was glad to see him enjoying the companionship of the older boy. Such activities filled his hours and reduced the pain of his mother's death. Ann, too, was glad for the time she spent helping Caleb Craighead with his school.

The Fletcher children were not much improved, however, and Caleb, who had gone below to see them, privately advised the parents quartered nearby to continue to keep their children as far away from the Fletchers as possible. Still, the fair weather was holding, and the mood of the passengers was optimistic.

"Ian said we could use his spyglass," Samuel told the girls one afternoon, "to see if we can find the other ships." Since the storm, the sails of the *Star* and *Regent* had been sighted infrequently, although the captain assured them that both ships had weathered it well and were reasonably close.

"Be careful," Ann called with a mother's concern as the boys began climbing the rigging of the mizzen-mast.

"Oh, look at them!" Isabel exclaimed as they watched their brothers scampering up the rope ladder like monkeys.

"Jonathan's not used to heights," Ann said anxiously, "I hope Ian is watching out for them."

"They're not likely to fall," Isabel shrugged, "but he could catch them if they did."

Samuel, looking through the spyglass aft of the ship, exclaimed that he could see a sail.

"The *Regent* be there," Ian said, pointing to the far horizon, "and summat t' port, the *Star* ."

"No," Samuel said, lowering the glass. "I can make out the lines well enough to see it's neither."

"Sail ahoy!" the lookout shouted from the crow's nest.

"What could that mean? He hasn't ever done that before," asked Isabel in alarm.

Immediately Ian ordered the boys to come down, took the spyglass from Samuel, and climbed up some ten feet, hanging onto the ropes with a practiced hand while he peered in the direction the lookout was pointing. By the time he returned to the deck, Captain Murdock had appeared, and he, too, surveyed the horizon.

"What do ye think it is?" Ann asked, but Samuel shook his head.

"I dunno. She's not flyin' any flag that I could see."

"Maybe it's a pirate ship!" Jonathan exclaimed.

"I most certainly hope not," Isabel said firmly.

"Go back to the main deck now, mates," Ian told them. "We'll soon know what the vessel be."

Hearing the commotion, some of the passengers stood about, shading their eyes and peering out to sea, but seeing nothing.

"Father, Samuel saw a ship!" Jonathan cried, running to William.

"So I heard. There be many ships in the Atlantic trade. 'Tis not unlikely that we'd chance to meet one from time to time."

"'Tis a good place for pirates to be, as well," Tom Prentiss murmured.

"Mid-ocean?"

"Why not?"

"But we are traveling with other ships," William pointed out, "and like us, they are armed."

"I can fight pirates," Jonathan said, earnest enough to bring a laugh from the men.

"Ah, lad, and I am sure ye could," William said fondly, "but that ship, if there is really one out there, is probably another merchantman, just as curious about us as we are about her."

A stir of activity on the wheel deck signaled that all was not well, and it was not long before the passengers realized their course had been altered. Still, nothing was visible on the horizon when the captain called for an assembly of the men on deck.

"We must assume the vessel is unfriendly since the we are not close enough to make out her colors. At present, however, we're in no danger. She seems to be making for the *Regent*."

"Is that why we changed direction?" Ann asked.

"No, daughter. We are making for the *Regent*, as well, and the *Star* is no doubt right behind us."

"The younger men are seeing to the magazine, just in case," Mr. Prentiss murmured under his breath to William.

But Jonathan overheard the exchange and jumped

34

up and down in excitement. "The magazine! Will they fire the cannon, then?"

"That will be done by the sailors if need be, son," William replied.

"What about us?" Isabel asked. "What are we to do?"

"Don't worry, lass," her father said. "There be weapons for the men to use, and the women and children will be safely below decks in case of trouble."

"But we aren't expecting any," William said quickly, seeing the alarm in Ann's eyes.

"All we can do now is wait," Tom Prentiss said, "and pray that the ship is friendly."

It was dusk before the familiar rigging of the *Regent*, which had veered in their direction, hove into view. Beyond it, some thought they could see the stark profile of a third vessel.

"Is that the *Star* following there?" William wondered.

Caleb, who had emerged from his meeting with the captain some time ago, shook his head.

"We were sailing in the middle of the three, so the *Star* is still to our starboard, unless she saw our maneuver and changed her own course."

Across the deck the first mate was scanning the seas with a spyglass, but could see nothing in the gathering gloom.

"By now someone should have made out that ship," Mary Prentiss said uneasily. "We ought to be told what is happening."

"The captain will tell us in his own good time," her husband replied. "We must be patient, and not think the worst."

"Come on, ye pirates! I'll give ye a fair fight!" Jonathan exclaimed, waving an imaginary broadsword.

"I think it is time the lad went below," William told

Ann, and when she moved toward him, she saw that his eyes seemed unnaturally bright.

"Let me stay up here," he pleaded. "I want to see the pirates."

"Jonathan, your face is very warm," Ann said, putting her hand to his cheek. "Do ye feel ill?"

"He got dizzy on the rigging," Samuel volunteered, but Jonathan insisted that nothing was amiss.

"I want to sleep on deck again," he said. "I don't like it below. It's hot, and there are strange shadows down there." The last few mild nights the children had been allowed to bring their pallets to the deck, a novelty they welcomed.

"Not tonight, Jonathan," William said firmly. "Go below and eat your supper. We'll have prayers presently, then ye must be abed."

CHAPTER 4

"I THINK JONATHAN MAY BE FEVERISH." Ann told Isabel when she returned to the deck.

"Maybe it's nothing," Isabel replied. "He was so excited today. But if that is a pirate ship out there . . ."

She broke off, and thoughts of pirates—looting, killing, marauding, kidnapping—troubled their minds.

"We are a poor lot," Ann said. "The Spanish ships would be better game."

"But the pirates have no way of knowing that," Isabel said. "Besides, poor as we are ourselves, the ship may carry a rich cargo, for all we know."

As the men dispersed from the captain's deck, Ann and Isabel stood waiting for their fathers to join them, eager to hear the latest speculation.

"Ye shouldn't be above deck," William cautioned. "Cap'n Murdock advises all women and children to stay below until further notice."

"Is it a pirate ship, then?"

"He fears so, since the vessel flies no flag. But he

hopes that our presence will prevent its attack on the *Regent*."

"In any case," Tom Prentiss added, "it is unlikely that anything will happen before dawn, and we are prepared."

"Will ye be armed?" Mary Prentiss asked fearfully, and her husband nodded and touched her arm in a comforting gesture.

"Where is Mr. Craighead?" Ann asked, suddenly realizing he was not among the men. Lately she had found herself noting his whereabouts, as if his presence were somehow reassuring.

"He stayed to meet further with the captain," William replied. "But come, now, 'tis pitch-dark, and ye need to get some rest. I'll see ye below."

When they reached their quarters, Jonathan was already asleep, but his face was flushed, and he was breathing harshly through his open mouth.

"I don't like the way he looks," Ann said, but William did not seem to share her concern.

"Likely it's just the excitement, and the boy will be fine tomorrow. I'll take a pallet up on deck and bed there tonight. Try not to worry," he added, but his own face was drawn and Ann knew that he, too, was missing Sarah, who would have known just what to do for the boy.

"Do ye think he has the fever like the Fletcher's bairns?" she asked Mrs. Prentiss when she dropped in to check on Jonathan.

"Might be," Mary Prentiss replied, laying a practiced hand on his brow. "Wet a cloth and wring it out and put it to his forehead to bring the fever 'round. Keep his lips dressed wi' lard—the sailors can give you some—and see that he has as much of water and gruel as ye can get down his gullet."

"How are the Fletchers?" Ann asked.

Mrs. Prentiss paused and shook her head. "'Tis hard to say. The little one is taken bad, I fear.

Jonathan may have the same fever, or he may not. In any case, most fevers will take care o' themselves in a few days time," she added, seeing that Ann was close to tears.

"Thank ye for the help," Ann said. "I'll see to getting the water now."

The sailor Ian immediately brought a basin of water and a lump of fat the size of a guinea egg, promising to see that she would have gruel for Jonathan whenever it was needed. Having done all she could for the moment, Ann lay on her bunk, sleeplessly awaiting the uncertain day ahead, and wishing with all her heart for her mother's calm and peaceful spirit.

At dawn, those who had been able to sleep awoke to the sound of distant cannon fire. In the darkness of night, the *Regent* had become separated from the *Derry Crown*, and was now apparently under attack by the unidentified ship.

Above them, Ann could hear the barking of orders and the shuffling of feet on the planking—then the thunder of their own cannon. Though the attacking ship was too far away for their fire to be effective, William had explained that the captain wanted to assure the *Regent* that help was forthcoming.

Jonathan awoke briefly and drank some water, but his fever remained high, and despite the noise and confusion, he seemed frighteningly unaware. Mrs. Prentiss stopped by to see how Jonathan was faring and confirmed the rumor that the Fletcher's infant daughter had died during the night.

"But the Fletcher boy's fever has broken, and he spoke this morning," she added brightly.

Ann nodded, taking small comfort in Mary Prentiss's words. She had watched her mother sicken and die, and now her brother was thrashing in delirium, his face red and his breathing labored. He turned his head when she tried to put wet cloths on his face, and

39

he would not swallow the gruel she offered. As the morning wore on, the quarters below deck became stifling, and one of the women opened the hatch above the stairway, heightening the sounds of the battle and confusion above.

"Ye look almost as flushed as Jonathan," Isabel told Ann when she brought her some bread and cheese at noon.

"It's the heat," Ann said, brushing damp tendrils of hair from her face with the back of her hand. "I'll be fine."

"You ought to walk about some, anyway. I'll sit with Jonathan for a time."

"Unfortunately, there isn't any place to go, but I will stand up and stretch a bit. What do ye suppose is happening out there?"

"From what I hear, I judge we are moving around the *Regent* now, so we can have a clear shot at the pirate ship."

"Then we might draw fire, as well."

"I suppose so. I don't think the pirates have boarded the *Regent*, although I heard someone say they were rigging a battering ram."

Ann shuddered. "And how are the others—the women and children? Seems I can hear nothing but the cannonade in the distance."

"Oh, you won't hear a thing out of anyone down here, I'll vow. We're all too frightened to do anything more than pray and wait!"

"I wish we could go on deck," Ann sighed. "Even a breath of air would help."

"Go to the top of the stairs, at least," Isabel urged. "You look fair done in."

As she stood, Ann managed a faint smile. "Maybe we can take turns breathing. There's hardly any air left."

As Ann reached the top of the stairs, there was the familiar sight of sailors heaving on the rigging.

Nothing seemed amiss, until she caught the glint of metal from the long knives stuck through their belts. Just then Mr. Craighead came into view. He, too, was armed with a brace of pistols. Ann was taxed to imagine his using a weapon, but at that moment the schoolmaster looked grimly determined enough to do so, at that.

"Mr. Craighead," Ann called softly, not wanting to give away her presence in a forbidden area. "Can ye stop for a moment?"

"Mistress Ann, don't ye know ye're in danger here?" But the tender expression on his face belied the stern tone of his voice. "And how are ye faring below? I know 'tis warm and likely to be warmer yet 'ere this day is ended."

"'Tis hot and close there, true enough, but we can stand it for a time. Did ye know that Jonathan is ill?"

"Your father said he might be. What ails him?"

"I think he must have caught the fever. The Fletcher bairn died in the night."

Caleb shook his head sadly. "I dinna know—I should be down there with them, but just now every man may be needed, and I must not leave."

"Can ye tell me what is happening?"

Caleb repeated the story Isabel had told Ann, adding that shortly they would be in firing range of the pirate ship. "If you hear anyone order the hatches shut, be certain to pull the bolt from the inside," he warned, "and stay away from the stairway. When you hear our cannon firing, go to your bunks and stay there. I'll come down as soon as I can. Will ye be all right?"

Ann wanted to say some brave words, but all she could manage was a nod, and with a touch of his hand to hers, Caleb walked away.

"You there! Away from the hatch!" the first mate called, seeing her at last.

"Things may soon be getting noisier, when our

cannon is fired," she told Isabel when she returned to their quarters.

"Noise is fine," Isabel said, tossing her head, "as long as I know who is making it."

An ear-splitting exchange of cannon fire, punctuated by much shouting and firing of smaller arms, convinced them that the pirates must be waging a full-scale attack. During a lull in the fighting one of the women— Ann could not tell just who—began reciting the twenty-third Psalm, and one by one, others joined in. Suddenly Ann recalled Caleb's warning about the hatch. She was halfway up the stairs to bolt the door when it opened, and Caleb himself bounded down the stairs toward her.

"Everything is fine," he assured them. "We have fired on the pirates and they are in retreat. The captain says ye are all to have an airing now, but ye must be ready to return below at a moment's notice."

The women and children needed no urging, but Ann hung back, eager for a word with Caleb.

"I must speak to the Fletchers," Caleb told Ann, "then I'll come back and see Jonathan."

She waited, hearing the murmur of his voice and the soft sobbing of the bereaved mother. Evidently Caleb had persuaded her to leave her sultry quarters, for she went out past Ann and up the stairs, and Caleb came to stand by Jonathan's bunk.

"He has been like this since last night," Ann said

Caleb put his hand on the boy's forehead, then on his chest, and shook his head. "Aye, he looks just as Danny Fletcher did at first, but Danny's much better now, and soon Jonathan will be, too."

"I have been putting wet cloths on his head, but the water is all gone. Can ye ask someone to bring more?"

"I'll see to it myself. But try to rest, lass. Ye look done in, yourself."

"If anything happens to Jonathan . . . after . . . "
She could not finish, nor did she try to stop the tears.

"I am going to ask God to spare Jonathan and to comfort and strengthen ye," Caleb said. "Will ye pray with me?"

Ann nodded, unable to speak for her tears, and kneeling by the bunk, Caleb began to pray. He asked for healing for Jonathan, safety for all of them during the remainder of their journey, and peace for Ann. "Amen," he finished, and rose to his feet. "I'll bring the water and sit with the boy so ye can go on deck awhile. I'll return soon."

Ann dried her tears, strangely moved by Caleb's prayer. His strength had flowed through her, lifting and warming her. Strangest of all, the peace he had prayed for seemed to be settling upon her. Then another part of Ann's consciousness acknowledged the man who had done the praying. No one in all her life had ever affected her so.

When Caleb returned with the water and took her place by Jonathan's side, Ann joined the other passengers crowding the rail. From the distance of several hundred yards that separated them from the *Regent* , Ann could see the smoke of several fires burning on the vessel's deck. Most of the ship's sails were down, whether from having burned or by plan, she could not tell. Beyond the *Regent*, she could barely make out another set of sails, but the pirate ship was now too far away for its guns to be any threat.

"How is Jonathan?" William asked anxiously, seeing Ann.

"About the same. Mr Craighead is with him now. Do ye think the pirates will return?"

"I doubt it, but we'll stay close by the *Regent* in case they do."

"It must have been fair sporting to see!" said Isabel, her vivid blue eyes sparkling.

"They are well-fitted to do battle," William replied, "but had we not been able to join her so soon, the

43

Regent would be in the pirates' hands, without a doubt."

Noting an edge of excitement in her father's voice, Ann realized that he had enjoyed the encounter with pirates. What was it about danger that men found so attractive?

"Ye all look so dangerous, with those knives and big pistols," Isabel said. "Were the transported men given arms, as well?"

"Yes, they were," her father answered. "There would be no reason to refuse them the right to defend themselves. Most of the men are being transported from debtor's prisons and were never ordinary criminals, anyway."

"And they'll be free in America, when we get there," William added.

'Well, not exactly," Tom Prentiss corrected. "They'll serve five years' indenture before they're on their own. But 'twould be against their own best interests to cause any trouble aboard ship."

"Mr. Craighead has done a good work with those men," William remarked. "He has them saying their prayers every night, I hear."

"He has been kind to *everyone*," Ann said, "and we mustn't take advantage of him. Father, I should go back to Jonathan now and let Mr. Craighead rest."

William glanced at the sky, which was rapidly darkening from the east. "We may all be joining ye soon. Looks as if our fair spell of weather may be coming to an end."

Thunder rumbled across the sky as if to confirm William's prediction.

"Thank God that's not cannon fire," Tom Prentiss said fervently.

"'Twill help put out the fires if it rains," Ann heard someone say as she went back to the stairway.

When she reached Jonathan's bunk, Ann saw that Caleb had fallen asleep, his head resting against the

44

bulwark. With eyes closed and face unguarded in sleep, the somewhat stern lines around his mouth were barely noticeable, and he looked younger— vulnerable now, and very human. For a long moment she studied those faint lines as if some vital secret might reveal itself there. For the first time it occurred to Ann that no one gave comfort to this man, who gave so much to others. Surely he must need encouragement sometimes, she thought. Or was his faith and trust in God so complete that it filled his whole life, with no need for anything or anyone else?

" 'Could ye not watch a little while?' " he quoted ruefully, opening his eyes and smiling at her in chagrin at being observed.

"Ye need to rest, too," she said, flustered, "Ye ought to go and get some food now."

"I will," he said, rising to his feet. "Send for me, though, if Jonathan seems worse or if ye need aught."

"We owe ye a great debt already—more than can ever be repaid."

"Nay," he protested. " 'Tis the other way 'round." Caleb put a hand to Ann's cheek for a moment and then, almost before she had time to realize he had touched her, he was gone.

Outside, the thunder crashed, and the ship began to roll as the wind freshened and the billowing waves rose. The storm broke, sending the women and children streaming back into the family quarters, but Ann scarcely noticed.

Isabel found her standing by Jonathan's bunk, her hand pressed to her face, her eyes staring into the distance.

'There'll be a rough night ahead," Isabel said. "Ye'd best get ready to hang on."

"Yes," Ann replied, "I will." She climbed into her bunk and watched the shadows deepen into darkness. This night, too, would pass. And tomorrow—tomorrow, she would see Caleb again.

CHAPTER 5

THE *DERRY CROWN* PITCHED AND TOSSED for two days, and once again Ann felt the wretchedness of seasickness. To her surprise, however, she began to recover even before the storm's fury was spent. William could take no food, but he stayed nearby, seeing to it that she and Jonathan had whatever was needed. Kegs had been placed on the deck to catch rainwater, and William, with Ian's help, brought down enough to their quarters to last for several days.

"The water that was put on at Londonderry is no longer fit to drink, but this is fresh," William said as he handed Ann a cup. "I'll lift the boy up, and you try to make him swallow a draught."

Despite the motion of the ship and Jonathan's restless thrashing, Ann was able to get a bit of the water down his throat. She took some comfort in the knowledge that Jonathan was at least no worse, a fact that Caleb Craighead confirmed on his visits. Because so many were now ill, he never stayed very long, but he stopped by several times a day, a calm and reassuring presence in the midst of the turmoil.

On the third morning, when the storm seemed to be waning, Ann awoke with the feeling that it would be a critical day for Jonathan's illness.

"How is he this morning?" asked Mary Prentiss, herself wobbly from seasickness, when she saw that Ann had opened the curtains around their bunks.

Ann laid her hand on Jonathan's cheek. His hair was matted and his eyes darkly circled, but his color was better. "He seems less feverish," she said cautiously.

Mrs. Prentiss nodded. "'Twas about this time that Danny Fletcher came to himself. Jonathan will surely do the same."

Ann said nothing. Neither of the women would utter the thought that was in both their minds—that during this same crisis period, the Fletcher's baby girl had died. Ann remembered too, so vaguely that she was not certain whether she had dreamed it, her mother's sitting at the bedside of two dead infants, clasping her Bible in her lap and never shedding a tear. In the hope of a measure of comfort, Ann took Sarah's Bible from the table and held it. Instead of consolation, however, it was a grim reminder of her mother's absence. Sarah would have known what to do. If she had not died, Jonathan might never have become ill at all. *I should have died*, Ann thought. *I should be ill now, instead of Jonathan*. So deeply was she absorbed in her dark thoughts that at first Ann did not realize Caleb was standing beside her.

"Are ye all right?" he asked.

Startled, she turned to face him. "Oh! I didn't know ye were there! I was woolgathering, I guess. . . . Jonathan looks some better this morning, don't ye think?"

William, who had gone for more water, returned with it and watched as Caleb touched the boy's forehead gently. "I don't know what we'd do if we lost him, Mr. Craighead," William said thickly.

47

It was the first time Ann had heard William admit the possibility that Jonathan might not recover. *If Mr. Craighead says we must accept God's will, I'll scream!* she thought.

"Let's pray together," he suggested, and knelt with them around Jonathan's bunk. As Caleb asked God to heal Jonathan and strengthen them all, Ann took her brother's hand, which now seemed but little warmer than her own. Had she imagined it, or had Jonathan's hand moved in hers? She opened her eyes as the prayer ended to find Jonathan, clear-eyed, regarding them with curiosity.

"What's the matter?" he asked, seeing that they were on their knees, and then, remembering, he sat up so suddenly that he almost struck his head on the bunk above. "The pirates! Are they still out there? Can I go see them?"

Ann sank back on her heels, tears of joy stinging her eyes.

William and Caleb both laughed, relieved, but Caleb answered the boy kindly. "No, Jonathan, I think the pirates have left us for better game. How do you feel?"

Jonathan lay back, his forehead suddenly damp with perspiration. "Tired," he said. "I would like some water, please."

Caleb touched Jonathan's forehead again and nodded. "God be praised, the boy's fever has broken."

"Don't take too much of this," William warned as Jonathan eagerly seized the cup of water he had poured. "Ye have not had much food or drink these several days, and too much now won't stay down."

"Several days?" Jonathan echoed, looking puzzled.

"Aye, son, ye had a long sleep, but with a bit of rest, ye'll soon be good as new."

"I had some strange dreams," Jonathan said, his face clouded. "I was with Mother up on Maunder Hill

48

just as the sun was going down. But then she went away, and everything got dark, and I was afraid. I called and called, but she didn't come back.''

"It's all right,'' Ann said, hugging Jonathan to her. ''That was just a bad dream. Rest and I'll see what I can find for ye to eat.''

"Thank ye for lookin' in on us,'' William said as Caleb got up to leave. ''The Lord most surely heard your prayers today.''

"No more than yours. Or . . .'' Caleb said, looking at Ann, ''yours. I must go now and tell the captain the good news. He has been much concerned about the boy.''

As Ann fed Jonathan some broth, her relief at his recovery was almost eclipsed by the pain that his mention of Sarah brought her. She would be here now, smiling at her son, if God had heard Ann's prayer.

"Ann?''

"Yes, Jonathan. What is it?''

"When I thought everybody had left me in the dark, I was scared. I know Mother won't be back, since she's in heaven, but I don't want you to go, too.''

"Hush, now,'' Ann soothed. ''Those were just feverish dreams ye had. Ye were never alone, not for a moment, and I promise that I'll never leave ye.''

Jonathan nodded, stretched, and yawned. ''All right,'' he said drowsily, ''but next time, wake me up. I wanted to see the pirates.''

When Ann was satisfied that Jonathan was sleeping peacefully, William sitting alongside, she ventured on deck for the first time in several days. The sky was clearing, with no sign of another sail anywhere on the horizon. A brisk wind was moving the *Derry Crown* along at a good pace.

"'Tis good to be out again, isn't it?'' Isabel greeted her. ''Mr. Craighead told us that Jonathan was mending—we are all greatly relieved.''

"As are we," Ann replied, "and I'm glad to see that the ship is underway again."

"We were blown off course in the storm, according to Ian, and no one has seen the other ships since."

"Including the pirates?"

"Yes, thank heaven. We lost a day's sailing maneuvering around the *Regent*, but with fair weather and a holding wind, we should make port in another ten days or so."

"This is our seventh week out, isn't it?" asked Ann, amazed she had not completely lost her sense of calendar time. "Father wasn't expecting that we would make port on the announced day, but I for one will be very glad to set my feet on dry land again."

"We may not be able to walk by then," Isabel smiled. "After the pitching of this deck, people may think we are tipsy." Then her expression grew serious, and Isabel squeezed Ann's hand. "I wish we could stay together when we reach America."

"So do I," Ann replied, "but our destination is uncertain."

"I have heard that the colonies are huge past all imagining, with more than enough room for everybody in Ireland and Scotland as well, but Father will go where a merchant is needed."

"And we'll be going wherever the land is available. We have the name of a wool merchant in Philadelphia, a man from our county, who can give Father advice."

"I doubt we'll stay in Philadelphia," Isabel said, "since it is a large city and already full of merchants. But I do hope we settle where people are nigh."

"So do I," Ann agreed, but in reality she had not given much thought to what would happen when they reached their destination.

Suddenly she realized that she was not looking forward to the end of the voyage. As tiring as the journey had been, as tragic the circumstances, there was at least a predictable pattern to their lives. In addition, the little community of passengers, with Caleb Craighead as their unofficial leader, had forged friendships, strengthened by the bond of shared hardships.

Resuming the threads of family life without her mother would be an overwhelming task. Ann knew that with the void left by Sarah's passing would come the burdens of everyday life. Would she be equal to the task? Physically, Ann knew her strength excelled her mother's, but Sarah had always relied on inner resources that gave her abilities beyond that dictated by her poor health. Ann hesitated to admit her fears, particularly to Isabel, who had obviously never concerned herself about spiritual matters. And certainly Caleb Craighead's faith seemed unshakeable.

Caleb resumed the children's lessons, once again enlisting the aid of Ann and Isabel, but she never saw him apart from the others. And so the days quickly passed, and Ann kept her thoughts to herself.

The weather held, the wind continued fair, and one morning Ann awoke to the sound of seagulls, come out to greet the ship, wheeling and calling above the sails. Everyone crowded to the rail, eagerly searching the horizon for their first glimpse of land, but it was not until that afternoon that the first faint smudge appeared on the western horizon.

"Is that Philadelphia?" asked Jonathan, who had been allowed to spend several hours each day on deck. He was still weak from the illness, but his curiosity was undiminished.

"No, lad," said Ian, overhearing Jonathan's question, "that land ye see is far to the north of where we're bound. Ye'll see that we'll turn more southerly now, and lay for Delaware Bay."

"When will we get there, then?" asked William.

"'Tis two days to the Bay, then we wait for the health inspector to row out to the boat and clear us to

51

land. After that, we come in with the wind and the tide."

"Will we see Indians in Philadelphia?" Jonathan asked.

"Ye're not likely to see any savages in the city," Ian replied, "but once in the country, ye'll see a few."

"We've heard that the Indians in Pennsylvania are a peaceful lot," William said. "I hope 'tis true."

"The Penns are always treatyin' with the Indians," Ian said. "Bein' Quakers, fightin' is agin' their religion, so mayhap they've worked a bit harder for peace than some of the other colonies. For my part, I don't rightly hanker t' live amongst 'em, though."

Overhearing the conversation, Caleb Craighead joined them. "I know the Penns, as proprietors of the colony, have always respected freedom of religious choice, as well," he said. "William Penn was a Quaker, yes, but he never set out to make it the religion everyone else had to follow."

"And where will ye be going when we land, Mr. Craighead?" asked William. "I don't believe we've heard ye say."

"I am not sure," the minister replied. "Since I am a redemptionist, I must raise my fare within three days of landing, or be indentured."

"Indentured! I should think the church would have paid your way, and gladly, with so many of us coming over these days."

"I did not ask it," he replied. "I can always earn my keep as a teacher, if it comes to that."

"But for a minister not to follow his calling—"

"I have reason to believe that certain ministers in Philadelphia will help me," Caleb interrupted. "In any case, I am already a servant of the Lord, and in His hands."

"What would your term of indenture be if ye can't raise your fare?"

"It depends on what the captain asks. For the men being transported, it is five years. In my case, I think he could get my fare for a three-year term."

"Three years!" exclaimed William, expressing a-loud the alarm that Ann felt on hearing Caleb's words. "'Tis a long time not to be your own man."

"'Ye are not your own, but have been bought with a price,'" he quoted from Scripture. "The Lord will provide," he added, and looked at Ann with an expression she could not fathom. "Utter trust comes only from utter dependence."

"A hard lesson," William murmured, shaking his head. "Jonathan looks tired, daughter. You had best take him below now. He ought not look peaked when the inspector sees him."

Ann did as she was told, picking up the light burden and starting for the stairs.

"I wish Mr. Craighead was coming with us," said Jonathan, to whom the talk of indenture meant nothing. "I feel lots safer when he is nearby."

"Aye," Ann agreed, thinking how well Jonathan had put it.

The man seemed to impart a quiet strength to all whom he touched. Certainly, of all the passengers aboard the *Derry Crown*, Caleb Craighead was the one man she would never forget.

CHAPTER 6

THERE WERE CHEERS FROM THE WEARY PASSENGERS of the *Derry Crown* when oceanbound colonial fishing vessels and merchant ships passed by, some so close that the features of those on board could be clearly seen. Then the *Regent* sailed by, bound for Charleston Harbor, and, in a few hours, the *Star*. As the ship neared the coast, they could make out houses and trees and could see spirals of smoke rising from cooking fires.

Two days later the *Derry Crown* lay at anchor just inside Delaware Bay, tantalizingly close to the city that was its destination. Those who ventured on deck with the first light of dawn were rewarded by the sight of the sun gleaming on distant red brick buildings and shimmering on newly leafed trees. As the city awoke, the ship's spyglass revealed a panorama of horses and wagons, herds of cattle being driven from the city to graze on common ground, dockworkers, sailors, merchants.

Now that their journey was over, Ann felt as though she could not endure another delay to feel dry land beneath her feet. Still, the ship could approach no nearer until the inspector gave his approval. Impatient, the passengers had packed up their belongings and they now stood, like so many refugees, at the rail.

As the hours passed and the inspector did not appear, Captain Murdock announced that a hearty meal would be served in the evening, as there were still ample rations.

"I certainly hope to be on shore before then," said Mary Prentiss. Like the others, she had packed her family's belongings and stood on the deck by the luggage, watching for the inspector's arrival.

"The captain seems easy enough about it," William remarked. "Ye would think he'd want to be about his business, as well."

"Ah, but the more that know the *Derry Crown* is landing, the better the crowd for the auction, when the unconsigned goods and the convicts are offered," Tom told them, passing along what he had heard Ian say. "Likely the notice will be posted today that we are in port."

"Then we'll not leave the ship today?" Mary Prentiss asked, disappointed.

"We could, if the inspector comes in time and approves it."

I wonder how they feel? mused Ann, looking at Caleb who was conversing with some of the men facing auction. "Do they know they are about to lose their freedom?" she asked aloud.

"Those men were prisoners," William reminded her, "and, besides, indenture isn't permanent. With a fair master, they'll be taken care of for their terms, and then have a fresh start."

"Still, it sounds like an uncertain business," Ann replied.

"Look!" called Jonathan, who had stationed himself at the rail with Ian's spyglass. "A boat is rowing this way."

"Here, let me look," said William, taking the glass.

A man, bewigged and looking quite official, was being conveyed by rowboat. Presently the portly gentleman, in flowered waistcoat and dark knee-breeches, clambered up the rope ladder that had been lowered for him. After disappearing into the captain's cabin, the inspector emerged some moments later waving a sheaf of papers and began a perusal of the sailors who had been mustered for his inspection.

"And are these all of your passengers? Are there any below?" he asked, glancing at the family groups gathered on the deck. Captain Murdock glanced inquiringly at Caleb, who nodded his head in confirmation.

"My passengers are all here, Dr. Elliott," the captain said. "Of course, you may check the quarters if you like."

Ann tensed, not knowing what to expect. There were few physicians in their part of Ireland, and to her memory, no one in her family had ever been attended by one. Even though the sun had put some color back into Jonathan's cheeks, and he was no longer running a fever, he did not look entirely well, and she feared the inspector's diagnosis.

She caught her breath when he paused before Jonathan.

"You, lad! Are you ill?"

"No, sir," said Jonathan faintly.

"Put out your tongue," the inspector directed. He tilted the boy's head, pulled up his eyelids, then put an ear to his chest before he was satisfied. "Captain Murdock, you must carry more victuals in your hold," he said, moving on to the next group. "I have seen scarecrows with more meat on their bones."

"He didn't ask about the fever," William whispered. "Now if he sees nothing amiss with Danny Fletcher, we should all pass."

Older and stronger than Jonathan, and with the

advantage of several more days of recuperation, Danny looked as well as the rest of the children. Everyone had lost weight and had come to think of their gaunt frames as normal. Only now, as the doctor scrutinized them, did Ann notice anew the prominence of hipbones and the hollowness of cheeks among the passengers.

In ten minutes more the surgeon general, having taken a quick look below the decks for form's sake, placed his seal on the passenger manifest and with a final wave for the captain, returned to his boat.

"When can we land?" The single question sprang from several throats.

"First tide tomorrow," Captain Murdock called to them, "if we've a bit of wind to help us. "Mr. Craighead, whilst we are all assembled, I think it would be fitting if ye would offer our thanks for a safe passage."

Even those who had not attended the Sabbath services fell to their knees as Caleb raised his arms and closed his eyes. The atmosphere was heavy with emotion as the passengers, soon to be parted, were united once more—in relief that the long voyage was over and in uncertainty of the future.

As Caleb called on God to continue to lead them on their separate paths, Ann wondered what the next days would bring for him. If he felt apprehensive about his own future, he gave no hint in his voice, which was firm and positive.

The prayer ended, and the passengers dispersed to prepare for their final night on board ship. Ann, remembering that she still had Mr. Craighead's copy of *The Pilgrim's Progress*, went below for it and returned to find him packing his books.

"I almost forgot to return this," Ann said, holding the book out to him.

"Did ye have an opportunity to finish it?" he asked, making no move to take it from her outstretched hand.

"I have not read it all," she confessed.

"Then keep it, and share it with others as you go," he said.

"Oh, I couldn't do that!" Ann protested, aware of the book's value. In Ireland, such a book would cost a working man half a month's wages.

"Sit down," Caleb invited, closing the lid of the box to make a seat. "Do ye know how this book came to be written?"

"I think Reverend Duffie told us it was written from a prison."

Caleb nodded. "Aye, John Bunyan spent twelve years in prison because he refused to stop preaching. Christian's search for the Celestial City represents our journey of life, with the temptations and problems everyone must face."

"From what I have read, it is a sad story," Ann said. "Everyone tries to stop Christian, or hurt him, and there are so few who are willing to help."

"Ah, yes, but did ye note the ending?"

When Ann shook her head, Caleb took the book from her, and quickly turning the pages, he began to read aloud:

Now I saw in my dream, that these two men went in at the gate; and lo, as they entered, they were transfigured; and they had raiment on that shone like gold . . . . Then I heard in my dream, that all the bells in the City rang again for joy; and that it was said unto them, "Enter ye into the joy of your Lord". . . . Now, just as the gates were opened to let in the men, I looked in after them; and behold, the City shone like the sun; the streets also were paved with gold; and in them walked many men, with crowns on their heads, palms in their hands, and golden harps to sing praises withal . . . .

Caleb closed the book. "The heavenly city is the end of Christian's journey. Just as we have reached the end of our voyage, having been beset by various woes, so one day when we reach the end of this life's

58

journey, will we go to claim God's promises. That is the message of this book." He held it out to her once more. "Please take it."

"I cannot accept it."

"Accept its message, then."

Ann dropped her eyes and felt the blood rushing to her face. While she was still attempting to frame a reply, Caleb spoke.

"Your mother knew that her family would grieve for her, and she asked me to give all of you what comfort I could. Your father has great resilience, and Jonathan, though a child, has fared well, with your help. But I have sensed that ye—"

Ann spoke quickly. "Ye have been a great help to us all," she answered him, meeting his level gaze with difficulty. She could not let him know how spiritually empty she was and risk his scorn, or worse, his pity.

"Not as much as I should have been," he said, "especially not for ye. I was hoping—"

"We are all most grateful to ye," she interrupted. "Please don't concern yourself about us. Whatever happens, we'll manage."

Caleb looked as if he would say more, but Ann turned and left him standing there, holding the book and gazing after her with an expression that would have surprised her, had she looked back.

There was little time for prolonged farewells the next day when the *Derry Crown* eased up to one of the new wooden docks that had just been built for the burgeoning Atlantic-West Indies trade. Except for Caleb and the men who were being transported, all of the passengers and their belongings were off the ship before nine o'clock.

The McKays and Prentisses shared the expense of a freight wagon to carry their luggage to the city. Ann, Isabel, and Samuel walked along beside it, while Jonathan was allowed to ride on the seat with the teamster.

"The grass here is not as green as in Ireland," Isabel noted as they passed a meadow where cows were grazing. A boy little older than Jonathan, attending the cattle with the aid of a long stick, waved to them, and Jonathan waved back.

"The soil does not seem to be so rocky, either," Ann observed. "Father always said that stones were Ireland's best crop."

"And the land is flat, as far as it can be seen." After passing a scattering of partially constructed buildings along Dock Street, the driver turned the wagon onto the widest street they had yet seen, with wooden market stalls and stores selling every kind of item imaginable. Although the roadway was unpaved and the sandy soil was already dusting the hems of their dresses, broad flagstones stood before each house, and most had hitching-posts set in them.

"Philadelphia certainly doesn't look much like Londonderry," Isabel said, comparing it to the only other city either of the girls had seen.

"The houses are finer than I expected," Ann said. Although there were some buildings constructed of stone and a few of wood, the majority seemed to be of brick made from red clay, a material seldom seen in their part of Ireland.

"Cap'n Murdock said we could lodge here cheaply and in comfort," Tom Prentiss said presently, ordering the drayman to stop before a two-story house, identified by a brightly colored signboard as the Swallow Inn. The owners were a Quaker couple who dressed plainly and whose speech was liberally sprinkled with "thee's" and "thou's," a novelty that greatly interested Jonathan.

After they had unloaded their luggage, William asked the way to the wool-merchant Josiah Pendleton's shop, and finding that it was but a short distance, decided to visit him at once.

"Ye'd best put Jonathan abed," he told Ann. "I'll see what the merchant advises."

Although he protested that he was not tired, Jonathan fell asleep almost instantly. Ann left the door open to their room and went across the hall to see Isabel.

"Let's go to the auction this afternoon," suggested Isabel. Tom Prentiss was readily persuaded to accompany them while his wife stayed at the Inn in case Jonathan should awaken.

A fair-sized crowd had already gathered when they reached the designated site, and Ann saw Captain Murdock's agent conversing with the men who would apparently conduct the sale. The cargo was put up first, and quickly sold. Then the agent appeared, accompanied by the men from the ship.

"Oh, look, there is Mr. Craighead, as well!" exclaimed Isabel, craning her neck for a better view.

"I thought he had three days to raise his fare," Ann said. "Surely the agent is not going to bring him to the block today."

"The sale has begun," Mr. Prentiss said, shushing the girls. They listened attentively as the agent read a claim that the first man was healthy and strong and had formerly worked in the stonecutting trade.

"Four pounds!" called a man with powdered hair and wearing a rust-colored velvet suit.

"Six pounds!" cried a gentleman with a wooden walking-stick and elegant silver-buckled shoes.

When no further bids were made, the auctioneer brought down his gavel. "Done!" he shouted.

The sale continued, until at last the agent pointed to Caleb Craighead.

"This man is a redemptionist," he said, "but he's a schoolmaster with a university education. Should any of ye want to pay his fare today, see me after the sale. If he's not redeemed, he'll be offered here day after next."

Even here, surrounded by strangers and in trying circumstances, Caleb had lost none of his quiet

61

assurance. Ann longed to go to him and speak some words of encouragement, but her action was unneeded. She watched as he bid farewell to the men whose fate he might well share, then made his way to where they stood.

"How awful—being inspected like a cargo of fish!" Isabel declared.

Caleb smiled at her indignation. "The agent was only doing his job," he told her. "It happens that schoolmasters with any sort of university education are in short supply in the colony, and he thinks I would fetch a good price."

"I don't see how ye can look so unconcerned, Mr. Craighead," Tom Prentiss said. "I'd think ye'd be on your knees asking for deliverance."

"The Lord is acquainted with my situation," he replied quietly.

"Well, _I_ still think 'tis a disgrace!" said Isabel, tossing her hair.

"Can you dine with us this evening? We are all staying at the Swallow Inn, just up a few blocks on Market Street," Mr. Prentiss invited.

"If I am back in time, I should very much like to join ye," he said. "I have been given leave to seek out some of my fellow ministers, and am to go to a place called Neshaminy. I have no notion how far it is, nor how long 'twill take to get there."

"May your errand be successful." Ann spoke for the first time. "If we were rich folk, we would pay your fare ourselves."

"There was some talk of it on the ship, but Mr. Craighead wouldna hear to it," Tom Prentiss said. "I still say if we'd all ha' given a bit, it could ha' been done."

"And I appreciated the offer greatly," Caleb replied, openly touched by Tom's sincerity. "Now if ye'll all excuse me, I must be about finding my way to Neshaminy."

"Poor Mr. Craighead," said Isabel as they walked back to the Inn. "What do ye suppose will happen if he can't raise his fare?"

"I don't know," Ann replied, wondering what would happen if he did.

William returned from Josiah Pendleton's shop just before the supper hour. As they ate, he told the others what he had learned.

"There's land to be had, all right, but not in these parts. Mr Pendleton suggested we head south and west—over the mountains."

"And is the land really free, as the agent claimed?" asked Tom Prentiss.

"Officially land fetches sixteen pounds an acre in the Pennsylvania colony, with a quitrent of a ha'penny an acre."

"That much!" exclaimed Ann, thinking of the slender sum that must support them in this new land.

"Aye," William explained, "but the quitrent is seldom collected on small acreage. It seems that the proprietors are so anxious to have land cleared and settled that they look the other way when squatters move in on an unoccupied grant."

"And how will you reach these lands?" Tom inquired.

"Mr. Pendleton said I should buy oxen and a cart here, since I'd have need of a team to clear the land when we arrive, and they're not to be found in the West. Then we travel to Lancaster."

"How far is that, Father?" asked Ann, wishing their journey would soon end.

"Several days hence," he replied. "First thing tomorrow I must see the merchants who can supply our needs. Mr. Pendleton was kind enough to give me directions and the names of men in Lancaster who can help us further."

Ann knew her mother would have felt Josiah

Pendleton's assistance was a sign that Providence was looking after them, and no doubt Caleb Craighead would agree. *If only I, too, could believe it*, she thought, *I might find peace*.

Caleb Craighead did not come to the Swallow Inn that Tuesday evening, and by Wednesday afternoon Ann had resigned herself to the probability that she would not see him again. The thought brought both relief and disappointment. On the one hand, she was afraid he would embarrass her by continually questioning her spiritual state; but at the same time, she longed to see him again. Something, she was not sure what, lay between them, unfinished.

Late Wednesday afternoon, when Jonathan was taking a nap and William and the Prentisses were gone to the Market, the indentured maid-of-all-work at the Swallow Inn knocked on Ann's door and announced there was a caller to see her.

It must be Caleb, Ann thought at once, feeling her pulse leap. Glancing at her reflection in the pier glass, she patted the bit of ribbon she had used to hold her hair back, and wondered if Mr. Craighead would find her appearance changed. She was wearing a dress of her mother's that had recently been altered to fit her, and thought perhaps it made her look older. Walking down the stairs she slowed her pace and tried to adopt a composure that would befit a more mature image.

Her efforts at entering the room gracefully were for naught, however, for Caleb stood with his back to the stairs. Hands behind him, he was looking out the window at the busy street and turned only when her heard her footsteps on the plank floor. When he saw her, he regarded her with some surprise in his clear gray eyes, and Ann's heart was wrenched at the signs of dust on his clothing and the lines of fatigue around his mouth.

"Everyone else has gone to the Market except

Jonathan, and he is asleep,'' she said quickly, already uncomfortable under his steady gaze.

"I am sorry to miss seeing them, but ye can tell them my news.''

"We have all been hoping that ye would raise the fare,'' she said and he nodded.

"That I have—with the help of Reverend William Tennant and some of his friends. He asked me to stay and teach in his college, but when he realized I felt a different call, he wanted to help.''

"Where will ye go then?''

"Where God has need of me,'' he answered simply. "Reverend Tennant mentioned that more and more settlers are venturing West, most of them with none to minister to them, so that direction would seem to be the most likely.''

"I am glad ye will not be indentured,'' Ann said. "We should not have wanted to see ye sold.''

"Nor I!'' he agreed. Caleb smiled, the quick upward lift of his mouth that only momentarily changed his usually sober expression, and Ann returned his smile, unable to think of anything to say to him. It was then that he reached into his cloak and brought out a small parcel, which he handed her.

"I want ye to take this,'' he said, "and make no argument,'' he added, seeing that she seemed ready to protest. "There is probably much that I ought to say to ye about God's dealings, but ye have heard it all before. The mind is often aware of a matter before the heart is ready to act upon it. My prayer for ye is that soon ye will find God's peace, as your mother did.''

Ann remained silent, holding the package he had given her and making no effort to return it. She had dreaded the time when Caleb would re-open this subject, dreaded even more the moment he would leave. And still she could not speak.

"Your mother loved you very much,'' he went on, "and just before she died, she asked me to look after ye. Although I am not in a position to do that now, I do not want to lose contact with your family. Do you know where ye will settle?"

"No, only that we will go west. The wool-merchant, Josiah Pendleton, told us to go to Lancaster and inquire there. We are to leave in the morning. Mr. Pendleton does business with many of our countrymen, and we are to tell him when we find a settling place."

"I will be in touch with him, then." Caleb reached out and took Ann's hand. "I have the conviction that we will meet again."

"Perhaps we will," Ann replied, making an effort to return his steady gaze. Still holding her hand, Caleb pulled her to him, pressing his lips to her forehead.

"Goodbye, child. God be with ye," he murmured, and was gone before she could speak. For a moment Ann considered calling after him, her arms longing to return his brief embrace. But he had called her "child," and Ann felt that she would be foolish, indeed, to believe that a mature man like Caleb Craighead could think of her otherwise.

Ann unwrapped the package he had given her, and found Caleb's copy of *The Pilgrim's Progress*. Opening the book, she saw that to his name and the words *Edinburgh, 1730*, had been added a fresh inscription: "For Ann McKay, whose pilgrimage is just beginning."

Ann closed the book and hugged it to her, happy to have something of Caleb's. It would be a talisman for her in the days ahead, she thought. And one day, perhaps it would bring him back to her.

When the others found that they had missed seeing Mr. Craighead, they were disappointed, but all were happy to hear that he would not have to be indentured. Although Ann did not tell anyone about Caleb's gift, Isabel apparently sensed that something had happened between them, and tried to find out what Ann was feeling.

"If Mr. Craighead already had a church, do ye think he would ask ye to marry him?" asked Isabel.

"Certainly not!" Ann replied, wondering where Isabel had gotten that notion. "For one thing, he thinks of me as a child, and in any case, with Father and Jonathan to look after, I've no time to be concerned with marrying anyone."

"You will, though. Over here, women are in short supply, and any girl can just about have her pick."

"Who told you that?" Ann asked, eager to steer the conversation into a neutral topic.

"Sally, the servant girl here at the Inn. Of course, she still has time left on her indenture, and can't marry until her term is up, but she says she's already had several offers."

Ann thought of the servant girl's pock-marked face and plain features and wondered if Sally had spoken truthfully. "Well, in that case," Ann said, "ye should have a husband and a houseful of bairns by the next time we meet."

"If only we could travel together!" Isabel said, growing serious. Tom Prentiss had decided to go down the Delaware River in search of a likely place to set up in trade, and, like William McKay, he did not yet know where he would settle.

"Father has his heart set on farming his own land, and when he makes up his mind to a thing, there's no way to turn him from it. It's unlikely that we would be in the same area."

"I know. But I'll miss having a friend like you to talk to."

"And we'll miss you all, as well," Ann replied, aware that she and Jonathan would both feel the loss of Mary Prentiss, who had become a second mother to them, and whose advice and aid would be sorely missed.

There were tears in Mary Prentiss's eyes that night as the families said their farewells. "Ye're a brave lass, and ye'll do fine on your own, I've no doubt," she told Ann. "Remember that your father may have to have your needs brought to his mind from time to time, not being used to managing without Sarah. Ye know that Jonathan is not well," she added, lowering her voice so that he would not hear her, "and when the hot weather fever comes, he'll bear close watching."

"I'll do my best," Ann replied. She had been surprised at the resilience of her brother's spirits, which had remained high despite the loss of his mother and the weakening effects of his illness, but she knew that he, too, would miss Mrs. Prentiss. And from all accounts, their land journey to Lancaster, a distance of some seventy miles, would be almost as arduous as the sea voyage had been, though not as lengthy.

"We'll not see ye in the morning," Tom Prentiss said at the door of the McKays' room as he paused to shake William's hand. "But Godspeed to ye all, and may we someday meet again."

"Amen," murmured William, and turned aside, unable to say more.

The wagon William had purchased to carry their goods to Lancaster was little more than a two-wheeled ox cart, and by the time their possessions were placed on it, there was barely enough room left for Jonathan. A bit of space remained at the rear of the cart where Ann could ride if she became too weary of walking, but she could tell even before she tried it that it would not be comfortable.

Jonathan was still half asleep when William brought him down at dawn, and hardly seemed aware of what was happening when he was placed in the cart. The early morning air was chill, and Ann wrapped a shawl about her head and shoulders as they walked through the waking city. William had been told to make his way to the western edge of Philadelphia to find the road to Lancaster, and with the rising sun behind them, they began the journey that would take them several days.

As they picked their way around the stumps and ruts of the Minqua Indian Path, they decided the Prentisses had been wise to travel by water. Walking along, each lost in thought, Ann wondered what was troubling her father. Never a jovial man, he had become moody and withdrawn since their arrival in Philadelphia.

"Father?"

"What is it?"

"How long do ye think it will take before we find our land?"

He was silent for a moment, then he shook his head. "The Lord only knows," he replied. "All we can do now is get to Lancaster. Then we must proceed from there on faith."

It was what Sarah might have said, Ann thought, but somehow William's voice did not ring with the same assurance.

CHAPTER 7

RAIN BEGAN FALLING EARLY in the morning of their second day on the road, and while the heavy canvas that William had bought in Philadelphia protected most of their belongings and kept Jonathan reasonably dry, the resulting quagmire slowed their progress considerably. Even her mother's boots and cloak couldn't keep the damp from crawling into Ann's very bones, and as the shower settled into a steady downpour and the air grew cooler, she wondered how long she could continue to walk. The sandy clay soil sucked at her feet, making every step an effort. Ahead of her, William walked by the oxen, the steam rising from their straining backs. From time to time he glanced in her direction, as if to assure himself that she was still there.

The land through which they had been passing had been settled for some time now. Already visible in the fields were greening shoots of buckwheat and other grains and occasionally Ann glimpsed a few houses and handsome stone barns. But gradually they had left the more populated countryside and were approaching an isolated section of road beside dense woods. For miles they met no other travelers, nor saw any sign of settlement.

William had been assured that there were no unfriendly Indians in those parts, but he kept an uneasy lookout nonetheless. The knowledge that William had bought a rifle in Philadelphia brought Ann little comfort. It lay wrapped in a protective cover in front of the cart. Before he could reach it, fill it with powder, and work the flint to fire a charge, she thought, even a lone Indian would have time to overpower him. Two or more would surely be able to kill them all. Ann shivered, as much in fear as from the cold. The *Derry Crown* passengers had made it abundantly clear—Indians could not be trusted, treaty or no treaty.

"'Tis a lone stretch," William said at length, when it seemed that they would never see open land again.

"Do ye suppose there might be an inn along the way? We canna spend the night in the wet like this."

"If we don't come to an inn soon, perhaps we can shelter in a barn like those we passed earlier. Are ye able to go on for now?" William asked, peering anxiously at Ann.

She nodded her head, sending a freshet of rain cascading from the hood of her cloak. "I can stand the weather, but I don't like the looks of this road. Suppose we met a highwayman?"

"Where is the highwayman?" Jonathan, presumed to be asleep, raised his head from the canvas and looked around expectantly.

"I was just making light," Ann said hastily. "There's no one else about, nor likely to be in this weather. Now put your head back under that canvas, before ye get a proper soaking."

"I'm hungry," he complained. "When are we going to eat?"

"When we get to a dry place. Here, chew on this,"

William said, tearing off a sinewy piece of beef jerky for the boy. He offered some to Ann, but she declined, having discovered the day before that it yielded very low returns for the time and energy spent on chewing it. Still, if it was all they could get, she would eventually have to eat it.

Perhaps another mile further, while negotiating a tight turn in the trail, they found themselves face-to-face with two young Indian braves, in long-sleeved shirts and leggings of deerskin, their heads bared to the weather. One carried a bundle of pelts, wrapped in a single deerskin and tied with a deerskin thong. Over one shoulder the other was holding a deerskin bag which Ann guessed to contain provisions.

William, warily eyeing the knives in their belts, made no move toward his weapon, but urged the oxen on. Ann prayed that the wheels of the cart would not choose that moment to mire down. But in making the turn in the trail, the oxen pulled too far to the side, and one of the wheels stopped, its forward progress arrested by a large stump. The snorting team halted, and Ann knew that it would take many minutes of tedious maneuvering to free the wheel. Such a thing was bad enough when the road was dry. Here, in the rain and mud and with the Indians looking on impassively, the vulnerability of the little wagon train was frightening.

"Get behind the cart and push," William directed. Ann, making a deliberate effort not to look at the intruders, did as she was told, but this time the ground was too muddy to afford traction, and she could exert no force. "Try again," William urged, prodding the oxen. From the corner of her eye Ann saw one of the Indians drop his bundle and take the knife from his belt, speaking something in a strange tongue to his companion.

"Look out, Father!" she cried, and Jonathan's head came up again, his eyes widening in surprise as he saw the Indians.

Still, William made no move toward his weapon.

The Indian turned and left the trail to enter the woods behind him, returning a short time later with several boughs cut from a long-leafed pine tree. As Ann backed away, he laid the branches under the cart wheel, and both he and his companion pushed, one on either side of the cart. The wheel hesitated momentarily before rolling over the boughs to a spot on the other side of the stump.

"We thank ye," William said to the man with the knife, speaking loudly as if that might help to make himself understood.

"You have trade?" the Indian with the pouch asked, pointing to the cart.

"I don't understand," William replied, shaking his head and speaking slowly.

"You trader?" the Indian asked.

"No, not a trader. I am a farmer."

At this both men laughed. "Squaw work," one of them said. "Better trade. Cloth, salt."

"We have some salt," Jonathan said, suddenly finding his tongue and the courage to use it.

"Hush!" Ann whispered, still unsure of what these savages might do with them. She hated to think what might happen if they lifted the canvas and found William's rifle.

"Ah," said the Indian with the pelts. "You trade— salt, fine beaver?"

"No," William said. "We have only a little salt, and we will be needing it ourselves."

The Indians conferred in their strange language, unlike any Ann had heard on the docks of Londonderry or Philadelphia, and apparently reached a decision. "No salt, no beaver," the one with the knife said, and Ann noted with relief that he had replaced the weapon in his belt.

"No trade," the other one said, and although he did not smile, neither Indian looked particularly menacing.

William called to the oxen, used his stick on their backs, and the cart lumbered on. Ann walked alongside, trying to make Jonathan stay under the canvas, but he sat rigidly upright, staring back at the Indians until they had disappeared around a bend in the trail.

"Our first Indians!" he exclaimed, having looked in vain for some in Philadelphia. "I wasn't a bit afraid of them, either."

"Put your head down, and should we see any others, do not speak to them," Ann instructed, trying to sound severe, but the relief in her voice was obvious.

"Mind your sister," William said sternly.

"They seemed friendly enough," Jonathan said, scooting back under the canvas. "I wish I had a shirt like that, and leggings, too."

"Perhaps ye will one of these days," Ann replied.

William cast a speculative glance about, and Ann knew that he, too, half-expected to see the Indians following them. Thinking of their knives, Ann hoped that they were not being stalked. She had heard tales of how skillfully an Indian could lift a man's scalp and the man live long enough to know the full horror of his death.

In the rain and the mud of that isolated trail, Ann suddenly felt very far from home, and very, very much alone.

Much to Jonathan's dismay and Ann's infinite relief, they saw no more Indians and few other travelers. At night they were able to shelter in stone barns near the trail, where sweet hay made a welcome bed. Its fragrance reminded Ann of their barn at home and she wept, remembering. Once a German farmer gave them food, and even though his words were strange, his message of hospitality was clear. *So,* Ann thought as they plodded along for what seemed to be forever, *there are good people in this land—people who help each other.*

Near Lancaster a trader with full beard and hair braided Indian-fashion, caught up with them. The man, who said his name was Paul Yancey, was leading two pack horses laden with goods he hoped to trade with Indians in return for pelts. He glanced at Jonathan, but his gaze lingering on Ann brought a blush to her cheeks.

"Where are ye bound with your goods?" William asked the trader.

"On to the southwest, to the banks of the Susquehanna River."

"And do ye find trading a better life than farming?"

"I'm no farmer, man," the trader said with a coarse laugh. "I learned that when I was indentured to a planter in Virginny. Soon as my time was out, I bought a few trinkets and set out a-sellin', which I been at ever since."

"Then ye must know the land hereabouts well. Is it all as fertile as this?"

The man nodded. "All the land that was easy to get to is taken up. To keep on goin' west, though, you have to cross mountains, and that's hard goin' for a team. It's bad enough for a man on foot with pack horses, like myself."

"But is there a road to follow?"

"Indian trails, maybe this wide," the trader said, gesturing with his hands. "There's no place you might ever want to go to that don't have an Indian trail leadin' to it."

"We're from Ulster, and I was told there was land beyond Lancaster a man could settle on without a grant."

"Donegallians, eh? I'm swanned if the Irish and the Dutch have any left to home at all, so many are comin' to Pennsylvania. Yes, the land beyond the ridges can be had, if yer not afeared o' Indians and hard work."

William described their encounter with the Indians.

"They wanted salt, but they didn't try to take it from us. Are the Indians really trustworthy?"

Mr. Yancey scratched at his stubby beard reflectively. "I didn't meet up with that pair, but as to whether Indians is friendly or not, I'd have to say yes and no, both. The ones around here have pretty much been forced out, what with the treaties takin' land they been usin' and all, an' most of 'em have gone on west. Some o' the ones there don't hold to no man's treaty, and ever' now and again, they go a-rampagin' against any whites they can find. They don't bother me none, though," he added, "'cause I got things they want."

"We were warned that it is best not to trust any savage," William said.

"Mebbe," Yancey agreed, "but I wouldn't turn my back on lots of white men I know, neither. There's some rough ones around, I can tell you that."

He left them near Lancaster, casting a final look at Ann. Ann's discomfort in no way resembled the feelings she had experienced when Caleb looked at her. Still, she wondered what this man would have said or done had not her father been with her.

Lancaster was larger than Ann had expected, and they had no problem finding an inn. After the German proprietor had seen to the animals and taken Ann and Jonathan to a room, Ann used the waning light to read from the book Caleb had given her. Her understanding was still lacking, but the knowledge that Caleb had often held this book, in hand and in heart, gave a small measure of comfort to the yawning uncertainty of the future. As she had so often in the past, Ann thought of Caleb, tried to imagine where he was and what he was doing. Above all, she wondered if she would, indeed, ever see him again.

CHAPTER 8

DURING THE THREE DAYS THEY STAYED at the inn, William talked with several men about his best course of action. His uncertainty increased with the information he gleaned. Striking out with a young girl and a frail boy, with no clear notion of where he was going or what he would do when he got there, suddenly seemed foolish.

Jonathan continued to look pale and hollow-eyed, and at night he often coughed. Although it was not mentioned, the sound of his coughing brought the chill suspicion that the boy might carry the sickness that had taken his mother.

Finally, after a second visit with James Andrews, a prosperous merchant who, while not an Ulsterman, was acquainted with Josiah Pendleton, William returned to the inn and announced that he had made his decision.

"James Andrews is a fine man, and he has made an offer that will be of great assistance to us."

"And what is that?" Ann knew from the way that William was pacing about the room that he was uncomfortable.

"Mr. Andrews' wife, Martha, is not well. He believes that ye might be a suitable companion for her. If so, he is willing to take ye and Jonathan into their home until such time as our plans are set."

"Ye would leave us here, and go on alone?" In all her idle speculation about the future, that possibility had never once occurred to Ann.

"It would only be for a short while, lass. Under the circumstances," and he paused, eyeing Jonathan playing quietly on the lawn, "I think it would be best for all of us."

"What is Mrs. Andrews like?" she asked resignedly.

"I have not met her myself, but I am sure she is a fine lady, and would be good to the both of ye. We are to call there directly, so ready yourself up and come along."

The Andrews house, like most of the dwellings in Lancaster, was of a single story, but the eight windows on the front of the house and the imported fanlight over the front door attested to the prosperity of its inhabitants.

Mr. Andrews answered the door himself and greeted them cordially. Ann immediately liked the man. His direct look and hearty manner were qualities Ann had always thought bespoke honesty.

When he conducted them into the sitting room, she found cheerful whitewashed walls and rich furnishings, including several pieces of upholstered furniture. Mrs. Andrews was sitting in a wing chair by the fireplace, a quilt covering her legs. In contrast to her husband's ruddy complexion, Mrs. Andrews was somewhat sallow, with dull, listless eyes. Her mouth, turned down at the corners, gave her the appearance of one who has just bitten into sour fruit, and she did not smile as she was introduced to the McKays.

"You, boy," she said, pointing a plump finger at Jonathan, "are you noisy?"

Perhaps because of her pronounced English accent, or perhaps because he did not understand her meaning, Jonathan did not immediately reply, and this seemed to irritate her. "I asked you a question, boy. Are you noisy?"

"Noisy?" Jonathan repeated, still unsure of what he should say.

"I cannot tolerate noise," she warned. "Most young boys are entirely too loud."

"Jonathan is a quiet lad," William said, putting a hand on the boy's shoulder. "He took a fever on the passage over and has not quite recovered his strength, but he will make ye no trouble, I can promise that."

Mrs. Andrews looked at Ann dubiously. "And you, mistress, are you strong enough to help me get about? I cannot walk without aid."

"I believe so," Ann replied, although she was far from certain. Mrs. Andrews was taller than Sarah, and more than a little on the plump side. Still, feeling that it was important to make a good impression for William's sake, she added, "I am stronger than I look."

"My daughter Elizabeth is about your size," she said, her eyes measuring Ann. "Since she married and went to live in England, I have been quite alone. My husband tells me that you can read and write. Is that so?"

Ann nodded. "Yes, ma'am, I can do both."

"And needlework?"

"I can spin and card, both flax and wool, and work a loom. I knit, but I've done no fancy work."

Mrs. Andrews sighed. "Well, I suppose if you can mend and fit material, that will be sufficient."

"Well, Martha, what about it?" asked her husband. "Will the girl do?"

"She looks frail to me," Mrs. Andrews said, as if Ann were not present, "but she does seem willing enough."

79

"Fine," said James Andrews. "Come along with me," he said to Ann and Jonathan, "and I'll show you around."

They followed him down a hall to a bedroom wing on the right, and he opened the door to a room at the rear of the house. "This was Elizabeth's room."

Jonathan, who had been cautioned before they left the inn not to speak unless he was directly addressed, appeared to be keeping quiet only with extreme difficulty. When he looked inside the small but sunny room, he could contain himself no longer. "Look, a real bed!" he cried when he saw the sturdy four-poster, strung with stout hemp, covered by a rolled-up feather mattress.

"There's a trundle underneath," Mr. Andrews said, pulling a small bed out onto the wide-planked flooring. The room had a few pegs on the walls for hanging clothes, a table with a candlestand next to the bed, and a chest bearing a basin and pitcher, over which was hung the rarest of luxuries in the colony, a real glass mirror.

"It's a very nice room," Ann said, trying not to stare at her reflection.

"The room across the hall belongs to our son, John," Mr. Andrews said, waving toward the closed door. "He is reading law in Philadelphia, so we seldom see him these days. Since the children left, and with having the fever of a summer, Martha hasn't been at all well." Looking at Ann, he added, "She needs the company of someone who can take her out of herself and cheer her up. Do you think you will be adequate to the task, Mistress McKay?"

"I will do my best," Ann replied, rather doubting that her best would be good enough to please Mrs. Andrews, but he nodded, seemingly satisfied.

"Come and see the rest of the house, then," he invited, and pointed toward the summer kitchen, detached from the main house for use in hot weather.

"Here is the regular kitchen," he said, leading them through a dining room with real chairs—not just backless plank benches—into a small, hot room where a huge brick fireplace almost filled the rear wall. A stout woman acknowledged their presence with a curt nod and continued to stir something simmering over the fire. The aroma of spices hung in the air, and Ann realized that she was hungry.

"This is Agnes, who does our cooking and cleaning," Mr. Andrews said. The woman's face was red, whether naturally or from the heat Ann could not tell, and her puckered mouth testified that she had lost most of her teeth. Her manner belied the somewhat fierce appearance she presented and, from the compassionate look she gave Jonathan, Ann knew he would have a friend in the kitchen.

As they returned to the sitting room, James Andrews asked William if he was satisfied with the arrangement, and he in turn looked at Ann. "How about it, daughter? Will ye bide with the Andrews for a time?"

"If I am acceptable to them."

"Then it is settled," Mr. Andrews said. "Martha, Mistress McKay has consented to stay with us." When his wife made no reply, James turned to William and shook his head. "I think it best that you bring their things over right away. This young man looks as if he could use a nap in his new bed, eh?"

Jonathan, realizing that William would not be staying there with them, burst into tears. Ann laid a comforting hand on his shoulder and led him from the room, hoping she might forget her own sorrow in trying to still his. Yet, when William brought their belongings from the inn, and was ready to move on, it was Jonathan who solemnly shook his father's hand, and Ann who clung to him, sobbing, until William gently pushed her away.

"Don't take on so, lass," he said. "I'll be back for

ye both as soon as I can. 'Tis but for a little while that we'll be apart.''

Ashamed, Ann dried her eyes and managed a weak smile, but as they stood in the doorway of the Andrews house and watched William walk away, Ann feared that it might be a very long time before they saw him again—if, indeed, they ever did.

Dealing with Mrs. Andrews was not as difficult as Ann had feared it would be, although it could hardly be called pleasant. She was expected to be at the woman's beck and call from breakfast until suppertime, except for a period in the afternoon when Mrs. Andrews rested. During those hours, when the house had to be absolutely quiet, Ann often took Jonathan outside as the weather permitted, and gradually extended their walks until they knew every street in Lancaster. After the evening meal, James Andrews usually sat with his wife, unless he had brought home guests, other merchants and artisans of Lancaster, or an occasional visitor from Philadelphia or London.

At such times Ann and Jonathan stayed in their room, and Ann finally finished reading *The Pilgrim's Progress*. She kept the book on her bedside table, along with Sarah's Bible. After a few weeks, feeling that Jonathan needed something to occupy his mind, she began to use the Bible to teach him to read, as she herself had been taught. But her efforts only called Caleb to mind and made her long to hear one of his comforting sermons.

She had learned of a church in Lancaster, with a native-born pastor, but Sundays proved to be the same as any other day to the Andrews, who, according to Agnes, were nominal members of the Anglican Church. Mr. Andrews often used the Sabbath for mysterious errands of his own, leaving Ann to perform her usual duties. Asking permission to attend church services seemed futile.

Ann and Jonathan tried to settle into the life of the Andrews household unobtrusively, but its ways were foreign to them, from the food they ate to the beds on which they slept. Jonathan sometimes had nightmares in which he would cry out for his mother, and Ann would lift him from the trundle bed and hold him until he fell asleep again.

Certainly Ann could not complain about their living conditions, by far the most luxurious she had ever experienced. The fare was hearty and rich, and, under Agnes' watchful eye, Jonathan gradually lost his gaunt look. Ann could only hope that it was a good sign, for he still coughed when he played too hard. But, having a neighboring boy to pass the time with, Jonathan was content enough.

Ann, too, had put on weight, so much that the dress she had worn on the ship no longer fit at all, and she cut it apart to make an outfit for Jonathan. The change did not escape Martha Andrews' attention, and one Saturday she had Agnes find a box of clothing left behind by Elizabeth.

"I notice that you seem to be outgrowing your clothes," she said. "These dresses should fit you."

"Will your daughter not some day want these things?" Ann asked, overwhelmed at the thought of having so many dresses at one time.

"Not these. Now that Elizabeth is living in England, she can have the best and the newest fashions. These would not be good enough for her, even if she should ever come back here, which is highly unlikely."

Ann put on a dress of the softest homespun wool, dyed with the precious indigo that was now being grown in the South Carolina colony, and stood before the mirror. From the tiny mother-of-pearl buttons on the fitted bodice to the deep flounce at the hem, the dress had an elegance that Ann had never seen, nor thought to have for her own. Regarding her reflection critically, Ann realized that just in the short time they had been with the Andrews, her girlish angular thinness had been replaced by a woman's softly rounded contours, accentuated now by the fit of the new dress.

"You look different," Jonathan said, coming in from outdoors.

"Well, I am," Ann smiled, turning to show off the dress. "I have three new dresses, just like a fine lady. What shall we do this afternoon?"

"David has some new kittens," he said. "I thought maybe we could go over and play with them."

"I don't believe I care to do that, but you may go. Just be careful not to track mud when ye come in. The ground's still soft from last night's rain, and we mustn't make extra work for Agnes."

After Jonathan left, Ann walked down the hall to Martha Andrews' room and knocked softly.

"Come in," she called, and Ann entered the dim room. The shutters were always tightly closed, even on the warmest of days.

"I thought I might take a walk this afternoon. Is there aught ye need before I leave?"

Mrs. Andrews sighed. "Well, if you are going to be about, find Mr. Andrews and tell him I am nearly out of my elixir. He can bring it home when he comes this evening."

"Yes, ma'am." Ann reached over to plump Mrs. Andrews' pillows and check to make sure she had fresh water.

"I see that you are wearing one of Elizabeth's dresses," Mrs. Andrews said. "It seems to fit you well enough."

"Yes, thank ye. Even Jonathan took notice of it."

Mrs. Andrews frowned and shifted her ample weight, rising on one elbow with some difficulty. "And he will not be the only male who does, I am certain. A woman walking alone on the streets may be misunderstood. Do not tarry on your errand, and speak to no one."

"No ma'am, I won't," Ann promised, but she was not sure she understood what Mrs. Andrews was trying to say. *She called me a woman,* Ann thought as she left the house, and the mirror had told her she had a woman's form. But inside, Ann still felt like a somewhat frightened little girl, and wondered when she might begin to feel that she had really grown up.

Ann found James Andrews at his place of business, and he stopped talking to his clerk to come around to the front of the office and greet her.

"It is well that Martha remembered the elixir today," James said when she had explained her errand. "Tomorrow I must go to Philadelphia, and it will be at least a week before I can conclude my business and return. Do you think that you and Agnes can care for Mrs. Andrews while I am away?"

"I am sure of it," Ann replied. "Tell me, will ye see Josiah Pendleton in Philadelphia, by any chance?"

"No doubt I will, as I have some business to transact with him."

"Then would ye please tell him that Jonathan and I are here in Lancaster at your home? He said we should let him know where we were, in case someone inquired."

"Certainly," he agreed, "although I wish I could also tell him where your father is. I take it that there has been no news today?"

"Nothing. It has only been a month, though," she added, "and he warned me that we must not grow impatient, as he expected it could take him some time to locate suitable land."

"Of course. I am sure he is fine. Now, if you'll excuse me, I'll see to the elixir."

Ann walked back to the house, unmindful of her surroundings. Usually she took pleasure in listening to the polygot population of Lancaster in conversation on street corners and around the marketplace, but today her mind was occupied with the possibility that, through Josiah Pendleton, Caleb Craighead might find out where she was, and seek her out. It was a frail hope, but all she had, and feeling that she was still very much a stranger in a strange land, Ann clung to it.

CHAPTER 9

WHEN JAMES ANDREWS RETURNED from Philadelphia, he brought welcome news.

"I saw John, and he is planning to pay us a visit within the week. It seems that Mr. Otis is going to New York to look at some property, and he gave John leave to come to Lancaster while he's gone."

"How did he seem?" Mrs. Andrews asked, with unaccustomed enthusiasm.

"He is well, but up to his eyebrows in debt," Mr. Andrews replied cheerfully. "I gave him a bit of cash, but I venture to say it'll soon be gone."

"He should not be in Philadelphia," Mrs. Andrews said. Her tone and the expression on her husband's face told Ann this was an old controversy. "I don't know why he couldn't have stayed here, since he wouldn't go to England and read at the Inns of the Temple."

"Now, Martha, you know there's hardly a lawyer fit to practice in this town, much less to teach anyone else the profession. When John finishes his studies, he may decide to come back here to practice, but in the meantime, you should be grateful that we see him from time to time. Had he gone to England, we would not have had that privilege.''

"He could come home more often," Martha pouted, but her petulance faded as she directed the household in a frenzy of cooking, cleaning, and polishing in honor of the impending visit.

"Ye'd think the governor himself was coming," Ann said to Agnes as she helped her put fresh linens on John's bed.

"Ah, that you would," Agnes agreed, "but he's always been fussed over. A little prince couldn't a' had more than that lad. He's a charmer, he is.''

"Have you been with the Andrews long?" Ann asked.

Agnes shook out a sheet and turned her head to one side, counting silently. "Well, lessee. I come here to work when the Andrews arrived, fresh off the boat from England. Must be nigh unto nine years now. Yes, Master John was eleven then, and Miss Elizabeth was going on ten.''

"What is John like?" Ann asked, but Agnes only shrugged.

"Like no one else you'll ever meet. You'll see.''

Still, Ann was unprepared for the laughing young man who flung himself into the house the next day and picked his mother up and whirled her around. Then he kissed Agnes, all before he had so much as set down his riding crop.

"And who is this?" he asked, turning from Agnes to see Jonathan regarding him with awe.

Ann had time to note the crisp blond hair, pulled back but unpowdered, and the well-tailored riding clothes. His smile, so unmistakably his father's, brightened what could, in repose, otherwise be a sullen expression.

"You remember my telling you about the McKays?" James said. "This is Master Jonathan, and this is your mother's companion, Mistress Ann.''

John turned to see Ann standing behind him, and she wondered if he recognized his sister's dress. Smiling broadly, John bowed from the waist and, taking her hand, kissed it. *"Enchanté,"* he murmured, and turned to his mother. "That is how one greets a lady in London, is it not, Mother? You always wanted me to acquire proper English manners."

"Your manners are far from English, whatever else they are," Martha said with some asperity. "A gentleman would leave his dusty cloak with the groom and clean his boots before he entered a house of quality."

John bowed. "Ah, I see you still know how to put me in my place," he said. "Excuse me, please, and I shall see to my horse. Young man—Jonathan, is it? Ah, yes, well, Jonathan, would you care to assist me?"

Enthralled, Jonathan followed him outside, and Ann helped Agnes take water to John's room. How strange, she thought, that the son was so unlike his parents in temperament. Even though John physically resembled his father, there was an air of recklessness about him that she could not imagine in James Andrews. And the way he had looked at her—it was not exactly the way the trader they had met on their way to Lancaster had looked at her, but it disturbed her nonetheless. Anyway, she told herself, John Andrews would soon be gone, and in the meanwhile, she resolved to stay out of his way.

Planning to avoid John Andrews proved to be easier said than done. One never knew when he would stay at home, talking to Martha, teasing Agnes, holding a skein for Ann, or showing Jonathan how to make a whistle from a blade of glass. He would leave at odd hours, sometimes just before meals, and some nights he would come in long after everyone else was in bed.

Four days after John's return, when the others were out and Martha was taking her afternoon nap, he surprised Ann at her loom in the summer kitchen wing. Quite certain that John knew she was alone, Ann tried to keep her eyes and her attention, on her work.

"What are you making?" he asked, taking a seat opposite her.

"Linen towels for the household," she said, holding the part she had finished up for his inspection.

"Very pretty," he said, not looking at the work, but at Ann. "What good luck that Fate put you on the Andrews doorstep. I can tell a great difference in my mother since my last visit."

Ann never knew how to respond to the infrequent compliments she received, so she said nothing. It didn't matter if John Andrews thought his mother's servant dull, she decided.

"Your mother's death must have been very difficult," he ventured.

She nodded. "Yes, it was."

"I'm sorry about your loss, but pleased with our gain. You and Jonathan have certainly brightened this house."

A cautious glance at John's face was rewarded by a broad smile. In spite of herself, Ann found that she, too, was smiling.

"That's more like it," he said, taking one of her hands. "You are quite lovely when you smile. You must smile more often—there, you've stopped. Come now, this won't do. Let's see that smile again."

In spite of her confusion, her lips turned up once more. This time, they were immediately covered by his, in a brief and gentle kiss. "A smile is much better than a grim mouth, don't you agree?" he said, dropping her hand and standing. "I promised Father I would look in on him this afternoon. I'll see you at supper tonight."

Ann sat immobile for some moments after he had left, reflecting on what had passed between them. The kiss had been brief, but it was her first, and the fact that she had enjoyed the touch of his lips on hers disturbed her. How could she face John again? She had made no protest, and Sarah's vague instructions concerning matters of romance had implied that a girl must not encourage a man's improper behavior. Was she guilty of such encouragement?

She almost decided to stay in her room during the evening meal, but she finally put on the buff linen dress that was her favorite and helped Martha Andrews to the table. John and his father arrived in time for John to seat his mother with a great deal of fuss.

During dinner he regaled her with so many amusing stories about Philadelphia that Mrs. Andrews neglected her food. At the meal's end, John and his father excused themselves to go to the Blue Boar Tavern, so Ann was not put in the awkward position of having to talk with him directly.

The next morning, at breakfast, John announced his impending departure for Philadelphia.

"You must stay at least one more day," Martha insisted. "We've hardly seen you the past few days, you've gadded about so much."

"Ah, Mother! Well, for you, maybe just one more day. What shall we do with it?"

"What do you usually do with your time and your money?" Martha asked making a great effort to look cross. "You waste it and then wonder where it went, and expect to be given more."

"You are a wonderful philosopher," John said, kissing his mother's cheek. "Mr. Franklin ought to copy your adages for his Almanack. I am quite willing to let you have the entire morning if I can have the afternoon."

"To do what?" Martha asked, smiling in spite of herself.

"I'd like to try my hand at fishing down by the Conestoga, and I'd like to take Jonathan and Miss McKay along. Have you ever put a line into the water, Jonathan?"

The boy shook his head, his eyes bright with excitement. "I would like to try it, though."

"And Father, how about you? Can you leave the gods of commerce long enough to practice the ancient angling arts with us?"

James smiled, but declined the invitation. "You know I have a shipment to get out today," he said. "A lawyer may be able to take a holiday whenever the fancy strikes him, but I must make a living. Go along, though, and enjoy yourselves. The river is lovely this time of year."

"Then it's settled," John declared. "Agnes, come out here."

"Yes, Master John?" She appeared from the kitchen, wiping her hands on her apron.

"Be ready to fry fish tonight, woman. With three sturdy anglers here, we should bring home an ample supply."

"Agnes sniffed. "That's as may be," she said, "but there'll be stew on the hob, nevertheless."

John returned his full attention to his mother. "Now, let me help you up, and we'll adjourn to the sitting room."

Ann stayed with Jonathan all the next morning so that mother and son could visit in private. Occasionally the sound of his laughter reached them through their closed door.

She was looking forward to their fishing expedition—though she had had no say in the matter—as a pleasant break from their normal routine and a treat for Jonathan. But also, she had to admit that she simply enjoyed being around John. His good humor and light manner lifted her spirits. On the other hand, she was not certain what he really thought of her, and she did not want to appear to be forward. She had chosen to wear one of her mother's dresses, not wanting to risk soiling any of her new things or appearing to dress up for him. But at the last moment before emerging from her room, she tied her hair back with her brightest ribbon.

"You say you have never fished before in your entire life?" John asked Jonathan as the three of them walked to the river at a leisurely pace.

"I went to the mill creek with Father once or twice, but I was too small to do aught but bait the hooks."

"And what about you, Mistress Ann? Are you as talented at fishing as you are at the loom?"

"Father never took me with him."

"Then I must teach you all there is to know," John said, and his look warned her that he might not only be talking about fishing. She tried to dismiss the faint prickling of apprehension associated with the memory of his lips touching hers, and resolved to focus her thoughts on the bright and pleasant day.

Reaching a shady and secluded spot that John pronounced acceptable they set down their creels and poles. Ann and Jonathan watched as John opened a packet of oiled paper and extracted some fat worms. "Let's see if the fish will find them as attractive as we do," John said, noting Ann's expression of repugnance. A farmer's daughter, she was no stranger to worms, but seeing them in a field that had been newly turned to the plow was quite different from picking them up and impaling their wriggling bodies on hooks.

"Here, Jonathan," John said, handing him a pole. "Sit down and let your line float in along the water. If you feel a tug on the pole, that means you have hooked a fish."

"What do I do then?" he asked, concentrating on holding onto the pole with both hands.

"Just pull it in gently—don't jerk it, or the fish will get away from you."

John repeated the hooking process for Ann, and motioned for her to take the pole. "Here, put your line out, not too close to Jonathan's." One of John's arms went around her waist, the other on her hand, helping her guide the pole into the water. He stood close to her a moment longer than necessary, then moved away to prepare his own line.

"Nothing is happening," Jonathan complained after only a few moments had passed.

"Shhh," whispered John. "You must be quiet, or all the fish will know that we are here. Be patient. One will find that juicy worm, then you'll have a nice fish to show Agnes."

After a few more minutes passed, Ann looked dubiously at John. "Are you sure there really are fish here?" she whispered.

"Trust me," he whispered in return. "In any case, it's a lovely day, and you're out of that stuffy house."

So he knows how it is, she thought. *He knows how difficult his mother can be, and he's doing this for me and Jonathan.* Ann felt a rush of gratitude at his kindness and smiled at him.

Just then Jonathan yelled, "A fish!" John quickly handed his pole to Ann and went to help the boy with his catch.

"It's awfully small,' Jonathan said when the fish was out of the water and lay flopping, gills heaving, on the grassy bank.

"Shall we throw him back in and wait for his big brother?" John asked.

"Oh, yes, let's do," said Ann, disturbed by the fish's imminent death.

John looked at Jonathan for instructions about the catch, and at the boy's shrug, he smiled and threw the fish back into the water.

"You are much too tender-hearted, Mistress Ann," John chided when they had all resumed their fishing.

Ann withheld her protests as other catches were made, and eventually they had caught five fair-sized trout. When their bait was exhausted, John and Ann put their poles down and sat side-by-side with their backs to a large willow that overhung the river bank and almost hid them from view. Jonathan had fallen asleep with the pole still clutched in his hand, and as far as they could see, no one else was in sight. Except for the quiet murmur of the river and the occasional call of a bird, all was quiet.

"I am not looking forward to returning to Philadelphia tomorrow," John said at length. He pulled down one of the willow branches and began absently stripping its leaves.

"Your parents will miss ye," Ann said. "Ye are the most important thing in your mother's life, ye know."

John made a gesture of dismissal with his hands. "More's the pity," he said. "She ought to live in Philadelphia, at least, or preferably, back in England. But Father thinks he can make his fortune here and then move back there. I hope he doesn't take too long to do it to help Mother."

"Why did your father come to the colonies?"

"My grandfather gave my Uncle Martin, the eldest son, all the land he had. He gave Uncle Paul, the second son, a ship, and he's in the Indies trade. He gave Father, the third son, enough money to start his business here, but Mother has never become acclimated."

"She is heavy," Ann ventured, choosing her words with care, "and that makes it hard for her to move about, but apart from that—"

"You've not yet seen her with the fever," John interrupted. "When it comes back upon her, it takes two strong men to tie her down on the bed—otherwise, she would shake so hard she might fall out onto the floor and injure herself. The fever seems to be associated with swampland, and once you have it, it doesn't let go. She'll need your help when the next spell hits her."

"When will that be?"

"Usually in the heat of the summer. Maybe in two or three weeks, maybe a month. When it comes, I hope you'll be strong enough to handle her."

"So do I," Ann said, her light mood shattered by his words. Mr. Andrews references to his wife's fever had been rather vague, giving no hint of its seriousness.

"Here, here," John said, taking one of Ann's hands and using his other hand to lift her chin. "That smile has disappeared again. We can't have that happen."

"I am concerned about your mother," she said, but she attempted a weak smile.

"That's much better," he murmured, and drew her face to his. This time his kiss was not brief. And when he put both his arms around her waist and held her closely, she encircled his neck with her arms and held them there until he released her.

"Ah, Ann," he said softly, "how sweet you are."

Suddenly embarrassed at her actions, Ann rose quickly to her feet, brushing at her skirt to hide her confusion. "Jonathan should not be lying in the damp grass," she said. "We must go home now."

"In a moment," John said, standing and reaching for her again This time he held her tightly without making any attempt to kiss her. "Will you be here when I come back?"

"I don't know," Ann replied, resisting the urge to add that she hoped she would be.

"Be here for me," he whispered urgently, and released her. He turned to pick up their gear and retrieve the fish they had caught. Ann gently awoke Jonathan. She and John said little on the way back to the house, and they were never alone again the rest of the evening.

The next morning, Ann awoke to hear muffled

96

farewells, and the sound of John's horse as he rode away.

"I hope John will come back soon," Jonathan said. "He said next time we could take a ride on one of Mr. Andrews' rafts."

"That would be nice," Ann said absently, remembering John's smile and the mingled pleasure and shame she felt as she thought of the touch of his lips. She knew that, somehow, she would never be the same again.

CHAPTER 10

"INDIANS . . . TOLLIVER STATION . . . killed three people . . ."

On her way to the market with Agnes, Ann stopped at the fringe of a knot of people gathered around a bearded man in deerskins. She had caught only a few words.

The growing crowd kept questioning him, but the trader threw up his hands and motioned toward the Blue Boar Tavern, where he had apparently been headed when the crowd stopped him. "Got to wet my whistle," he called out. "I've tol' yer all I know, anyhow."

The trader went inside, with some of the men following, but most remained where they were, talking among themselves about the news he had brought. Agnes saw a woman she knew and asked her what had happened.

"Injun trouble," the woman replied, and spat disdainfully. "Some hot-blood Irish out to Tolliver Station killed a brave and his squaw, for no good reason but the sport, it seems. Next day some Injuns came in and burned three cabins down the creek and took some scalps.''

"Who were they?" Ann asked.

"He didn't say, but I sure wouldn't want to be nowhere near that place, no siree.''

"Where is Tolliver Station?" Ann asked Agnes.

"Somewhere west o'here, on t'other side of the mountains. Don't worry none about Injuns, though,'' she added. "Here in town, yer safe as a baby in a cradle.''

"It's not myself I'm worried about,'' Ann replied looking toward the tavern. 'I think I recognized the man who was talking,'' Ann said. "We met him on the trail. He might know if Father was involved. I've got to ask him.''

"Yer can't go into the tavern, missy!" Agnes exclaimed.

"Then I'll just stand here and wait until he comes out.''

"That might take all day,'' said Agnes, "and yer can't stand about here alone.''

"Then go inside with me, Agnes.''

"Mrs. Andrews would have my hide if she knew of it.''

"Well, we won't tell her,'' Ann declared, starting for the door. "I must find out if he has seen Father.''

The Blue Boar Tavern featured a high bar and plank tables and benches in a large front room, with small private dining areas in the rear, where the gentlemen of the city could do their drinking and gaming in relative privacy. The trader stood at the bar, holding a pewter tankard. Along with every other man in the place, he looked up with interest as Ann and Agnes entered.

"Well, well, here are some mighty thirsty females, for sure,'' someone yelled, and there was a great deal of shuffling and laughter.

While Agnes sent glaring darts in several directions,

Ann ingored everything else and walked straight to the trader. "Mr. Yancey? I believe ye may remember seeing my father with my brother and me on the road into town some few weeks back."

The trader looked at Ann appreciatively, his eyes moving up and down in a lingering glance that brought the blood to her face. "Sure, Missy, I don't forget no faces. It 'pears like you've put on a mite o'flesh since then, eh?"

"I heard what ye said about Indian trouble at Tolliver Station. I was wondering if ye might happen to have seen my father again, or heard aught about him."

"Yer pa ain't here in Lancaster?"

"She is under the protection of James Andrews," Agnes put in quickly, seeing the man's lecherous leer.

"And yer father?"

"He left about six weeks ago to look for a place to live. He has not contacted us since. I hoped ye might remember seeing him along the way somewhere."

"No, but when I go back, I might ask around, as a favor to a purty gal."

The man was insufferable, but Ann tried to ignore his attitude. If he had any information about her father, or could procure any, he must be tolerated.

"The people the Indians killed—do ye know their names?"

"Perkins, I think it was, Irish folks like you, red-haired. Man and wife and one other, grown boy or man who happened by there, no one knew for sure."

"Thank ye," Ann said, aware that Agnes was plucking at her sleeve, impatient to be gone.

"Any time, missy," he said. "Tell y'what, I'll look yer up next trip, and mebbe you and me can have a little fun, eh?"

"That's an evil man, Miss Ann," Agnes said darkly, as they made their way outside. "If ever he shows his face around the house, he'll be sent packing in a hurry."

"I don't like him, either, but he may be able to find out where Father is. I am beginning to be worried that something terrible has happened, or he would at least have sent a message to us."

"Ah, that's easier said than done," Agnes told her. "There's no regular post through Lancaster, and with fever season upon us, folks don't travel more'n they have to. You'll hear in good time."

"I hope ye're right," Ann said. John had told her that his mother's fever attacks were severe, but until now, it had not occurred to her that one of them might also become ill.

As June wore on, the weather grew warmer than even the hottest days in Ireland. Ann watched Jonathan anxiously for any sign of sickness. Mrs. Andrews showed no signs of fever, but as the heat increased, her bulk and relative immobility caused her great discomfort. She became more irritable than usual, finding fault with everything and everyone that chanced her way.

So at first when she asked Ann for her shawl, in spite of the heat, Ann was convinced she was only demanding more attention. Nevertheless, at the woman's insistence she rose to retrieve the shawl, and when she returned she found Mrs. Andrews in the throes of a hard chill—the signal that the dreaded fever had once again recurred. A surgeon was hastily summoned, and as Ann watched his leeches gorging themselves on Martha Andrews' blood, she was thankful there had been no surgeon aboard the *Derry Crown* to give Jonathan the standard fever treatment.

She, Agnes, and Mr. Andrews worked to secure the delirious woman's arms to prevent her from injuring herself, and Ann began caring for her day and night.

At length the violent stage of the illness spent itself, and Martha Andrews was pronounced out of immediate danger. Mr. Andrews took over the close watch on his wife, and urged Ann to get some needed rest.

Walking to her room, Ann put a hand to the small of her back and stretched, trying to ease the pain of muscles kept too long in one position. She opened the door carefully, not wanting to disturb Jonathan's rest, and stood by his bed for a moment, suddenly overwhelmed by her love for him.

Ann slipped out of her dress and decided to lie down in her petticoat and take a short nap. The heavy feather bed had nearly smothered her when the warmer weather came, and Agnes had replaced it with one filled with cornhusks. It made a cooler bed, but a noisy one, and as Ann cautiously eased down onto it, the crackling of the husks woke Jonathan.

"I wondered where you were," he said, stretching and sitting up. "I dreamed that Father came back, and he had Mother with him, and we were all going somewhere wonderful in a big coach with four white horses. Then I woke up, and it was dark, and you weren't here."

"I was with Mrs. Andrews all night, but she is better. Ye must be quiet now, and perhaps ye can go back to sleep."

"Agnes said I should not make any noise and that I must say a prayer for Mrs. Andrews' soul. I tried to be quiet, but I didn't know how to pray for anybody's soul. I was afraid I might make her die."

He looked so woebegone that Ann gathered him into her arms and hugged him. "Ye have been a very good boy to be quiet and stay out of the way. But it would not have been your fault if Mrs. Andrews was worse. Such things are not in our control."

"I prayed for Mother, as hard as I could, and she just kept getting sicker."

"It wasn't your fault," Ann said. "Didn't Mr. Craighead talk to ye about it?"

Jonathan nodded. "I liked Mr. Craighead. I wish he would come to see us."

"Perhaps he will," she said, quietly. "Now let's lie very still and rest, shall we?"

Ann laid Jonathan back in his trundle bed and lay down again. When she closed her eyes, she saw Caleb as he had stood before her in the Inn. "I have the conviction we will meet again," he had said. Drowsily she thought that Josiah Pendleton could have told him where she was, if he had wanted to know. All she could do now was wait . . . for her father, for Caleb Craighead, for John Andrews . . . .

"The post rider brought this today from Philadelphia, James Andrews said to Ann, handing her a letter. "I knew you would want to have it right away, so I brought it over. Is Martha resting?"

"Yes, she has had a rather difficult day," Ann replied as she took a slender folded paper from his hand. She had never before received a letter of her very own, and in her haste to break the seal and open it, she tore a corner of the page. The writing was clear and neat, instantly recognizable as Caleb Craighead's hand. Five days had passed from the date he had written at the top of the page. She read:

> Dear Mistress McKay:
>
> I have this day called upon Mr. Josiah Pendleton, who has given me the intelligence that you are residing in Lancaster. He thought that perhaps by now your father would have found his land and made arrangements for you and Jonathan to join him. In any case, it is my hope that Mr. Andrews, in whose care I send this, will know where you have gone, and can direct me to you.
>
> The Lord has greatly blessed my efforts in Philadelphia, and I shall have much to tell you when I reach Lancaster, the latter part of the month.
>
> In the meanwhile, it is my prayer that you and Jonathan are well and happy in God's care."

"I hope that your news is pleasant," James Andrews said when he saw that she had finished reading the letter. He had politely withdrawn with his copy of the newspaper, but as she tucked the letter into her apron pocket, he put aside the *Pennsylvania Gazette* and looked at her.

"Yes, thank you. It is from the Reverend Caleb Craighead, who befriended us on the voyage over. He will be coming to Lancaster soon, he says. He kept a school on the ship—Jonathan will be glad to see him again."

"And, I wager, so will you," he said, noting her pleased expression. "You say that he is a school master? We could use him in Lancaster, then. My children had a tutor, but most of the young ones are growing up almost totally illiterate—a great shame. Tell me, does he plan to settle here?"

"It is my understanding that he intends to go on to the new settlements where there are few ministers as of yet."

"Well, there's no money in that," Mr. Andrews declared, "but I do business with several men who trade six days and preach on the seventh, and manage both quite well."

"I doubt that Mr. Craighead would make a merchant," Ann said, smiling faintly at the thought.

"Still, he should know about the possibility," Mr. Andrews said. "He would be serving people two ways, and a man could do worse."

"Thank ye for bringing the letter. If ye will excuse me, I must find Jonathan and share this news. He could use some cheering."

Over the next few days, Ann read and re-read Caleb's letter until she knew it by heart. She was almost afraid to meet him again. She knew that her physical appearance had changed in their months apart, in a way that any man was likely to admire. But her spiritual state, which had concerned him so much, was virtually unchanged.

With Mr. Andrews' permission, she had recently

started going to hear the Reverend Mr. Alexander preach on the Sabbath. American-born and poorly educated, he knew neither Hebrew nor Greek, and his sermons tended to be dull and repetitious. Yet she saw to it that Jonathan was enrolled in the catechism class, and each day she spent a portion of their prayer time in quizzing him on it. The catechism reminded her anew of the beliefs their mother had held so dearly, and which she could understand on an intellectual level.

But there was a measure of belief that she had not achieved, a plane of her existence that was not satisfied. Most of the time she was able to put it from her mind, but she felt sure that once he looked into her eyes in that penetrating way he had, Caleb was bound to know that she still lacked her mother's faith.

That evening, after Jonathan had said his prayer and was asleep, Ann took her mother's Bible from the table, and by the dim light of the single candle, turned to the Gospel of Matthew, and began reading.

Never had time passed more slowly. The heat had been aggravated by drought, and everything baked in the relentless sun. Agnes kept the kitchen garden alive with the aid of gallons of well water, drawn and applied with a gourd dipper early each morning. No one could work out-of-doors by suppertime, for the mosquitoes that had hatched earlier in the wet season made a vicious, biting attack on any foolish enough to venture outside. Ann had grown to dread their singing around her ears in the night, a sure sign that she and Jonathan would awaken the next morning to new itching welts. The goose grease that Agnes gave them to use as an ointment was messy and rank, but Ann used it and insisted that Jonathan do so, too.

"No one told us how hot it gets in America," Ann said to Agnes one morning as she was helping her weed the garden. "Or about these pests," she added, slapping at a persistent sweat bee.

"That's so," Agnes agreed, "but still I'd not trade places and be back in the hovel I come from, and that's a fact."

"I shouldn't complain, either," Ann admitted. "I know there was no future for us in Ireland, nor likely there would ever be. But I do miss the old ways and the old places, and I miss having the family together most of all."

"What you need is a husband," Agnes said with her grimace that passed for a smile. "Yer must be close to eighteen already, or I miss a good guess."

"I'll be eighteen in September," Ann said.

"Ann! Agnes! Where is everyone?" Mrs. Andrews called from the house, and Ann rose hastily, wiping her hands on the light shift she wore for outdoor work.

"Coming, Mrs. Andrews," she called back. "She'll be wanting her breakfast now, Agnes. Ye had best stop that and have it ready directly."

Agnes straightened up with difficulty and groaned, holding her back. "I'm too old to be doin' a man's work," she muttered. "Mr. Andrews ought to buy indenture papers on a man-o'-all-work t' help us out."

"Perhaps he will if ye keep reminding him of it," Ann suggested.

"Have you been outside again without your bonnet?" Mrs. Andrews asked by way of greeting.

"Yes, but the sun was barely up when we started working, and I had no need of it. Then we were so busy with our weeding that it slipped my mind."

"Humph!" Martha Andrews exclaimed. "Seems to me you find it convenient to let it slip your mind entirely too much. A young lady must not allow her skin to become discolored, and yours is dangerously close to that condition already."

"Yes, ma'am," Ann said meekly, having learned long ago that diplomatic agreement was the wisest way to handle Mrs. Andrews' notions.

While Martha rested that afternoon, Ann filled a basin with cool well water and sponged her perspiring body, exchanging the shapeless shift for the lightest of Elizabeth's cast-offs, a fine lawn dress in soft rose. In deference to the heat, she piled her hair atop her head, holding it with three tortoise-shell combs that Elizabeth had left behind. A few damp tendrils of hair curled around her face, softening it. Looking at her refelction, Ann found herself wanting Caleb to see her as she was now—no longer a skinny young girl, but a maturing woman. She smiled at her reflection, but the result seemed stilted and artificial. Her natural expression was good enough, she decided. If John found it too serious for his liking, she doubted that Caleb would.

CHAPTER 11

"IT'S MR. CRAIGHEAD!" Jonathan cried in the late afternoon of the following day. "He's here!"

Martha Andrews covered her ears and glared at Jonathan. "For heaven's sakes, boy, do calm yourself!" she admonished.

"Yes, Jonathan, slow down," Ann said, so occupied with soothing him that Caleb was well into the room before she saw him. Her first impression was that she had forgotten what a striking figure he made, then she realized that she was seeing him in clerical dress for the first time. His black coat and square white linen stock were were quite befitting the quiet dignity with which he greeted Mrs. Andrews.

"I do apologize for this intrusion, madam," he said, giving her his full attention and bowing formally. "It was certainly not my intention to disturb your household."

Somewhat mollified by his tone, Martha Andrews held out her hand. "You must be the minister Mistress McKay has been telling us about. She mentioned that the boy was looking forward to seeing you again."

"And I was hoping to see him, as well," Caleb replied, laying a hand gently on Jonathan's head.

"Have you come from Philadelphia today?" Mrs. Andrews asked.

"No, I stopped yesterday at Donegal, where I delivered some messages to a minister there. Today I came into Lancaster and left my belongings with the Reverend Alexander, where I shall bide tonight."

"I do hope you are free to take the evening meal with us," Mrs. Andrews said.

"It is kind of ye to invite me," Caleb said. "I'll accept the hospitality with thanks."

"Very well. Ann, if you will assist me, I will speak to Agnes."

"Yes, ma'am," Ann said, and with some assistance from Caleb, conducted Mrs. Andrews to the kitchen, grateful that she was giving them some time alone.

As Ann returned to the sitting room, Caleb was still standing, listening as Jonathan told a rather embellished version of their meeting with the Indians on the Lancaster trail. Caleb looked at Ann with a slightly amused expression, but she could see no hint that he had noticed any difference in her.

"Please sit down," she invited, and Caleb took the large chair with carved arms, deeply upholstered in maroon velvet, usually occupied by Mr. Andrews. Jonathan sat on the floor at his feet, and Ann took her usual seat, a comfortable Windsor chair, the only one in the room completely without upholstery.

"From what Jonathan has been telling me, ye have had several adventures since last we met," Caleb said.

"Most of them were in the getting here. Except for the few weeks when Mrs. Andrews was ill with the shaking fever, our lives here have been quite calm."

"And your father? What have ye heard from him?"

Ann shook her head, her expression sober. "Nothing. About a month ago I asked a trader we met to see

109

what he could find out, but he has not contacted me, either."

"David Zimmer says the Injuns prob'ly have him, is why we've not heard," Jonathan said earnestly.

"Your friend has a good imagination," Ann replied. "I am quite sure there is a good reason for his silence that has nothing to do with Indians."

"No doubt you are right," Caleb murmured, and quickly changed the subject. "I am glad to see ye both looking as if ye have fully recovered from the rigors of our voyage."

"Yes, we have an abundance of good food to eat here, and so far we have both escaped the summer fevers."

"Reverend Alexander tells me that the Andrews household is among the finest in Lancaster, but I have observed that even the most ordinary households in the colony set a good table. It is truly a blessed land, and everyone I have met has been most gracious.

"I wish ye'd stay here," Jonathan said. "I like ye lots better than Reverend Alexander."

"Jonathan!" Ann exclaimed.

Caleb smiled slightly, but his tone was firm when he spoke to Jonathan. "Reverend Alexander is a fine man, and he takes his duties quite seriously. He told me that ye attended preaching services and his catechism class, and I am glad to hear it. Remember that we do not attend a service to honor the minister, but the God whom he serves."

"Yes, sir," Jonathan murmured, somewhat chastened. "but I'll always like ye best."

"Your letter mentioned that ye had much to tell us," Ann prompted. "Does that mean ye have raised the funds ye need?"

"Well, as I mentioned, people have been most generous. I stayed with Reverend Isaac Drumlie, a man I knew at Edinburgh, and through his introductions I was able to visit many churches in the

Philadelphia area. The people, not being forced to pay a tithe to any religion, are more generous to the causes of the church than any I have ever known. From the collections that were taken on my behalf, I have been able to buy both a pack horse and a riding horse, with enough funds to sustain me until I am settled."

"And have ye determined where that will be?"

"Not exactly, but I have no doubt that God is leading me to a place of service in the western lands. By all accounts, there are hundreds of our people who have taken up grants in those areas and have no one to minister to them. When I come to such a group, there will I bide."

"Perhaps as ye travel ye can inquire about Father," Ann said hopefully.

"I shall do that," he promised, "and when I do see William, I know he will be relieved to hear how well ye both are."

Just then, Agnes called Jonathan to run an errand for her, and as soon as they were alone, Ann felt her old shyness and discomfort returning. She could think of nothing to say. After a moment, he broke the silence.

"'Tis true that Jonathan looks like a different lad," he began, "but I must also add that I perceive that ye, too, have experienced a change, Mistress Ann. Ye cannot have had a light burden here, with William away and in a strange new land, yet I sense that ye are far calmer and at ease with yourself than before. Ye wear that new responsibility well."

As she listened to him speak, Ann felt ashamed that she had thought Caleb would remark on her physical appearance. He still spoke to her as a minister to one of his flock, not as a man to a woman.

"I have tried to be brave, for Jonathan's sake, but there have been many times when I fear that he will become ill again, or that something has happened to

Father and we will see him no more. Lately I have tried to read the Bible, and have had prayer with Jonathan each night. For a long time, I couldn't bring myself to read the passages that Mother loved so much. I am trying to get over that.''

"Ye must continue to study the Word and to seek to do God's will. Your mother set a most excellent example for ye, and now ye must do the same for Jonathan.''

"I know,'' Ann replied, unable to bring herself to promise more.

"While we have this time alone, there is another matter that I wish to discuss,'' Caleb began, but was interrupted by the arrival of James Andrews. Ann had scarcely completed making the introductions when Agnes announced that the evening meal was served, and they adjourned to the dining room.

Agnes had already placed the food on the table, not the elaborate fare that might be prepared for the special guests that Mr. Andrews entertained for business reasons, but what would have been considered a feast in Ireland. In addition to thin slices of pink ham, there were side dishes of new potatoes in cream, tender garden peas, fragrant cheese, and a tray of pickles and relishes. This was served with crisp corncakes and buttermilk, cool from the cellar. A sponge cake waited on the serving board for dessert.

"I can certainly see why the McKays look so well,'' Caleb commented after being asked to return thanks for the meal. "A nobleman could not provide a better board.''

Martha Andrews warmed to Caleb's compliments and soon began to regale him with questions about Philadelphia.

"Our son, John, is reading law with Mr. Otis on Fourth Street,'' she said. "Perhaps you might have noted their establishment?''

"Is it in the vicinity of Arch Street? The Reverend

Drumlie showed me a magnificent public hall that Mr. Franklin and some of his friends—Mr. Otis among them, I believe—are building at Fourth and Arch Streets so that preachers of any religious persuasion will be able to address the people of Philadelphia. I thought it quite a remarkable achievement."

"No doubt it is," Mrs. Andrews replied, "but I fear that such an invitation may well be abused. When there are too many who claim to be preachers, the people tend to confusion. It seems to me that there is more harmony in a place with one established church and one belief, to which all men subscribe."

"There are many such towns within the colonies, but I am told that almost any religious persuasion can be found in the city of Philadelphia, and that all are equally tolerated."

"That is why many people came to the Pennsylvania colony in the first place, Martha," Mr. Andrews said, aware that Caleb Craighead did not need a lecture on the merits of a state church. "Lancaster has many faiths, too, Mr. Craighead. I should think that a man of your education would prefer to stay in Philadelphia, or even settle here, rather than to rush off to the wilderness."

"I was not city-born, and I would miss the freedom of being close to the out-of-doors. I suppose that is one reason that America appealed to me."

"You would be welcome enough in this town as a school master," Mr. Andrews said, "but if you are determined to go on to the western lands, might you consider becoming a trader, at least until you have a church organized? I employ several men who have done that, and with great success."

"I believe that the Lord will provide," Caleb replied, "and so far, He has not called me to be a merchant. If He does, I am certainly willing to try it."

"Do you really believe that God calls people to their professions, Reverend Craighead?" Martha Andrews asked, her tone dubious.

113

"I believe that there is a plan for every life, Mrs. Andrews. The happiest people are those who, whatever their occupations or stations in life, have yielded themselves to His will and operate within it."

"And what of those who are not of the flock?" Mr. Andrews asked. "Can they never be happy?"

"They may appear to be, and may even believe that they are happy, but in fact they are the most miserable of all men, for they have no hope of possessing eternal life."

"Reverend Craighead was invited to dine with us, not to dispute theology," Mrs. Andrews said, stirring uncomfortably.

"Sometimes I think talk of religion or politics ought to be universally banned around the dining table," said Mr. Andrews with a smile. "Will you have a slice of this excellent sponge cake, Reverend?"

"Thank ye," said Caleb, "but I fear I have already had more than I should. The meal was most enjoyable, and I appreciate your hospitality."

"I must bid you a good evening," Martha Andrews said, "and ask Mistress McKay to assist me to my room. But please stay on as long as you wish, and come again whenever you are in Lancaster."

"I must return to the Reverend Alexander's before dark," Caleb replied, "but first I should like to spend some time with Jonathan."

"Certainly," agreed James Andrews. "You and the boy may have full use of the sitting room."

"I feel unwell," Martha Andrews complained after Ann had helped her into bed. "See if you can find some fresh mint leaves for my indigestion."

Obediently Ann went outside, where already the lengthening shadows foretold that the day was almost done, and picked several sprigs of mint from the garden, washing them in water she drew from the well. The rest of the bucket she brought into Mrs. Andrews' bedroom and used to fill her bedside pitcher. "Is there anything else I can do for ye?" Ann asked, hoping that there would not be.

"I suppose not," Mrs. Andrews sighed, "and in any case, I can see that you long to be sitting with your minister. He's a handsome man, I grant you that, although he could use a more pleasant manner. You ought to persuade him to stay here and keep a school, instead of traipsing off into the wilderness."

Jonathan tells me that he is quite a fisherman," Caleb said, rising as Ann entered the sitting room.

"He has gone once, when John Andrews was here, but the size of his catch seems to increase with the passage of time."

"It was kind of him to give ye both an outing," Caleb said, rather formally.

"Next time John comes, he is going to take us for a raft ride on the river," Jonathan confided.

"That could be dangerous if ye don't swim," Caleb replied. "I hope young Mr. Andrews will exercise caution." Glancing at Ann, he added, "He seems to be a bit reckless."

Before Ann could respond, Caleb added, "Reverend Alexander will be anxious if I stay longer."

"Will ye come again tomorrow?" Jonathan asked.

"No, lad. I'll be on my way in the morning."

"Should ye come across Father—" Ann began, but seeing that she was close to tears, Caleb interrupted.

"I'll make inquiries as I go," he assured her. "In any case, I have not forgotten my promise to your mother, and until ye are all settled, I'll keep in touch."

"Was there something else ye had to tell us?" Ann forced herself to ask, seeing that Caleb was determined to leave. He looked at her with an expression she could not quite identify—sorrow, or disappointment, perhaps—and shook his head.

"No, not now. Perhaps the next time we meet,

when we are all more certain of our course." He put his hand to hers for a brief moment, murmured "God bless ye both," and left the house. Jonathan walked with him to the street, and Ann watched numbly as Caleb lifted the boy in his arms and kissed his forehead, then strode away without a backward glance.

"Why are ye crying?" asked Jonathan when he returned.

"Because . . . " Ann said, and stopped, not fully able to understand what had happened, but aware that something had gone terribly wrong.

"Are ye sad that Mr. Craighead is leaving?"

"Yes, I am. I had expected that he would stay in Lancaster for a few days."

"I wish he would, too. We talked some about it."

Ann wiped her eyes and looked at Jonathan, a suspicion slowly dawning.

"Just what did ye and Mr. Craighead discuss whilst I was gone?"

"First we talked about the catechism, and he said I was doing well on the memorizing but didn't know some of it perfectly yet. He asked me how I liked Lancaster, and I told him about my friends, and about John."

"What did ye say about John Andrews? I know ye told him about the fishing trip, but what else did ye say?"

"That we liked him, and that I hoped he would come back soon."

"Is that all?"

Jonathan looked uncomfortable and did not speak for a moment.

"Jonathan, what else did ye tell him?"

"Just that he kissed you some," he admitted.

"Oh, Jonathan!" Ann exclaimed, in anger and frustration. It was apparent that her brother had only pretended to be asleep the day they went to the river.

But to tell Caleb . . . no wonder he had seemed so distant.

"Are ye angry with me?" he asked, seeing her distress.

"Ye should not have said that, Jonathan. Ye know that Master John is full of high spirits and likes to tease. He kissed me because it was a fine day and we were all very happy. It was wrong for ye to pretend that ye were asleep, too."

Jonathan's eyes brimmed with tears. "I'm sorry," he said contritely. "I was just playing a game. I didn't mean to hurt ye."

"I know ye didn't," Ann said, her anger replaced by humiliation, "but I am afraid that Mr. Craighead must have a very poor impression of me now."

"I don't see why," Jonathan said. "What does that have to do with his being our friend?"

"He is still our friend, but ye must learn to hold your tongue in the future." She sighed and added, "What's done is done, and there is no need to worry about it. Now wash your face and get ready for bed, and let's say no more about what happened tonight."

Had Jonathan's thoughtless words spoiled any chance for something more than friendship between her and Caleb? What would he have said to her, had Jonathan remained quiet? Ann lay awake far into the night, pondering the questions along with the bitter realization that Caleb was more important to her than she had realized. More important than he would possibly ever believe.

CHAPTER 12

ANN AWOKE AFTER A FITFUL SLEEP to find that the sky was just lightening toward dawn. She lay still for a few moments. *I just can't let him leave with the wrong notion*, Ann told herself. Once resolved, she hastily drew on her clothes, and holding her slippers in one hand, tiptoed out of the house, taking care to avoid the floorboards that always squeaked underfoot. She was not sure what she would say to him, but she did not want their relationship to depend solely on a promise he had made to her dying mother.

Cutting through the dew-drenched lawn to the rear alleyway, Ann hurriedly covered the distance to the church, meeting no one along the way. The Reverend Alexander's home was a log house beside the church, and even with several additions and glazed windows, it was a far more humble dwelling than most of the houses in Lancaster.

The sun was breaking through a ragged fringe of orange-tinted clouds as Ann went to the rear of the house, where a rough shed sheltered the livestock. The grass showed signs of having been walked upon recently, and fresh hoof marks led to the street. There was no sign of Caleb or his pack horse anywhere.

Ann leaned wearily against the side of the shed. She was too late. Caleb had gone, and she had missed the opportunity to speak to him once more.

"Who goes there?" a voice called, and Ann looked up to see Mrs. Alexander standing at the rear door of the house.

"It's Ann McKay," she called back. "Has Mr. Craighead gone?"

"My, yes, with the first light," she replied. "But come inside and have a bit of breakfast with us." Mrs. Alexander held the door open for her. The minister's wife was wearing a severely-cut gray dress, the only color Ann had ever seen her wear. The Alexanders, both in their early forties, Ann judged, had three lively children who were apparently still sleeping.

"I can't stay to eat, but I'm obliged to ye for the invitation. I had hoped for a word with Mr. Craighead before he left."

"I believe you met one another on the voyage over from Ireland, did you not, Miss McKay?" the Reverend Alexander asked. In his plain morning clothes, and without his clerical collar, he could have passed for an ordinary laborer.

"Yes, and his presence meant a great deal to all of us on the vessel. He intends to look out for my father as he goes west."

Reverend Alexander poured his coffee into a saucer and blew on it, taking a swallow before speaking again. "Are you sure you'll not join us?" he asked. "Our fare is plain, but there is quite enough."

Ann looked at the coarse bread he was crumbling into curdled milk. "No thank ye. I should go now. I'm sorry to disturb ye so early in the morning."

"Nonsense," Jane Alexander said. Both she and her husband were natives of the colony, and they spoke in a somewhat flat, nasal tone that she sometimes had trouble understanding. "I'm just sorry you missed your minister."

"So am I," Ann replied. "Do you have any idea how far he'll have to travel to find a congregation?"

The Reverend looked amused. "He'll not find a congregation waiting for him anywhere, far or near," he told her. "Those who go west are settling on four hundred acre grants or double grants if they buy their land. Some parts are thickly settled, but many are not. People have taken up land all the way from the Delaware to the Susquehanna and in every direction in between, mostly following the Indian trails and the creeks. He could stop almost anywhere and find people who needed him."

"Do ye suppose Mr. Craighead will be letting ye know when he finds his stopping place?" Ann asked.

"He may," the Reverend said, looking keenly at Ann, "but I've no doubt that he will be in touch with you, in any case."

Mrs. Alexander smiled and looked knowingly at Ann. "Mr. Craighead asked us to keep an eye out for you and your brother in his absence."

"When did he say that?"

"This morning, just as he left," Mrs. Alexander replied. "He seems to be a true man of God, filled with the Spirit and anointed to preach the Gospel, but when it comes down to it, he can't do his best alone. He needs a helpmeet."

"That is quite true," Reverend Alexander said, nodding in agreement. "A minister needs a good wife by his side. Our doctrine teaches that celibacy is dishonoring to women and dangerous to men. Mr. Craighead is aware of that obligation; we discussed it with him yesterday."

Ann felt her face grow warm. Mrs. Alexander gave her a knowing smile "Don't you be concerned about Mr. Craighead," she said, following Ann to the door. "If the Lord is in it, he'll be back."

120

If only I could have seen him, Ann thought, as she walked back to the Andrews' house. The uncertainties of her life were becoming increasingly difficult to her. Mrs. Alexander had meant to be comforting when she said Ann would see Caleb again if the Lord were in it, but there was no solace there for her. "I am not good enough to be his wife," she said aloud, and the admission brought tears to her eyes. "What a mess I have made of things!"

Three days later, while Ann was carding flax and Agnes had taken Jonathan with her to the market, a dirty-faced boy, little older than her brother, came to the kitchen door and asked to see Mistress McKay.

"What is it that ye want?" Ann asked, thinking that the boy could use a hot meal and a good scrubbing.

"Are yer Mistress McKay?" he asked, peering in for a closer look.

"Yes."

"I have a message for yer," he said, "in private."

"Come inside," Ann invited. 'Would ye like something to eat?"

"No'm," the boy mumbled. "I'm not to come inside, but t'tell yer t'come wi' me now, if yer want word o' yer father."

"Who sent ye?" Ann asked, feeling a surge of hope.

"I ain't allowed ter say," the boy replied. "Yer t'come wi' me now," he added, as she hesitated.

"I must let Mrs. Andrews know I am leaving," she said. "At least tell me where we are going."

The boy shook his head. "Yer t'come wi' me now, and none's ter know," he repeated stubbornly.

"All right," she agreed, looking out to see if there was any sign of Agnes and Jonathan, but the alleyway they usually took to the market was empty. "Wait and I'll get my bonnet."

Martha Andrews was taking her afternoon rest, and

Ann decided not to risk disturbing her, and hoped she would not be needed before her return. Taking her bonnet from its peg, Ann walked out into the heat of the summer afternoon.

"What is your name, boy?" Ann asked as they walked down the alley, away from town.

"Tad," he replied, volunteering no other information. He led Ann toward the river where John Andrews had taken them fishing. As they passed the last house, Ann became increasingly uneasy.

"How much farther are we going?"

"Just down t' the ferry," Tad said, pointing. "See it?"

Up ahead on a wide expanse of the river, a flat barge, poled by a large black man, was slowly drifting toward the opposite side. A crude shed, built of rough-barked logs, stood on the near bank of the Conestoga, and the boy indicated that she should enter it. No one else was in sight, and the boy turned back toward town, his mission apparently concluded. For a moment Ann considered running after him, but having come this far, and wanting news of her father, curiosity overcame her fear, and she walked to the cabin.

"Come in, Missy," a male voice called as she reached the door, and she recognized it as belonging to the trader Yancey. He sat sprawled on a puncheon bench inside the cabin, bottle in hand, dressed in a soiled white linen shirt, open nearly to the waist, and ragged breeches.

"Why didn't ye come to the house?" Ann asked, standing just outside and casting an anxious eye toward the raftsman, who had just reached the opposite bank. She wondered if a scream would carry across the river, and feared it might not.

"Ah, missy, surely yer can see that I ain't dressed for town," he said, chuckling. "Besides, we can visit here a whole lot better, and nobody'll know our business."

"If ye have some news of my father, I would very much like it," Ann said nervously, and again he laughed.

"I'll just bet yer would," he said, "but first, come on in out o' that hot sun."

As she gingerly entered the cabin, he stood and held out the bottle to her. "This is prime rum—have some."

"No, thank ye," Ann replied, wishing that Yancey were sober. "Now, what do ye know about my father?"

"Well, Missy," he began, "I had ter go out of my usual way on my last trip, had some trouble with my lead horse. A blacksmith told me there was a passel o' Irish around Shawnee Creek that was down with the fever, so many that some were lyin' unburied. Some of the Shawnee Kishacoquillas come through that way and found 'em."

"What does that have to do with my father? Do ye know that he was one of the sick?"

"The smith didn't know no names," he said, and took another swallow from the bottle before continuing. "But I saw a cart that looked like the one yer pa had when he come here to Lancaster. When I asked the man where he got it, he said he bought it off an Injun. I figure it was likely stole from yer Pa."

Ann felt stunned, and she wondered if she dared believe his words. "There must be many ox carts like ours," she said, slowly. "By itself, that doesn't mean anything."

"Have yer heard from your pa, then?" he asked, moving closer. Ann backed away and did not answer.

"I thought not," he said, draining the bottle and wiping his mouth with the back of his hand.

"How can I find out for sure?" she asked.

"Likely yer could find somebody around Shawnee Creek that's seen the cart, and probably yer pa, too."

"Where is this place?"

"That's hard ter say. If yer take the Conewago Creek trail ter Tolliver Station and then turn south and follow Shawnee Creek fer a day, yer'll come to the blacksmith. He can tell yer from there."

"How long ago were ye there?"

The trader seemed to be having trouble reckoning the time, finally holding up five fingers. "This many days," he said. "If all goes accordin' to plan, I'll rest up a while and restock and head out again. Thought yer might like to go with me, Missy."

Ann was silent, wanting to turn and run from the disgusting man. But if he could help her find her father, she did not want to antagonize him.

"I must think about it," she said.

"Yer can't let old man Andrews know," he warned. "He'd tie yer up afore he'd let yer go with me, and that's a fact."

"He promised my father that he would look after us," Ann said, aware that the trader's words were likely true.

Yancey laughed. "That's a joke. There ne'er was a bigger crook in the Colony than James Andrews. Respectable as the Sabbath, he is, and crafty as a serpent."

She ignored his assessment. "If my brother and I went with you—"

"Not the boy," he interrupted. "He stays here, or you don't go, neither."

She paused. "If I decided to go with you, then there must be certain conditions on your part, as well."

"Of course," he said. "Yer'll find that Paul Yancey is a man o' his word, even if I ain't a fancy gentleman. Tell you what, Missy. You think over what I said, and let me know in a day or so. 'Twould be out o' me way to go back to Shawnee Creek, but I feel a bit sorry fer yer, and I'd see that you got there safe. Word'll get ter me at the Red Lion, just outside town. I won't be here long, though—don't miss yer chance."

In another moment Ann was safely out of the cabin, and she hurried back to the Andrews' house, her mind in a turmoil.

When Ann arrived, her duties kept her occupied until Agnes had the evening meal prepared. Ann had resolved to tell James Andrews about her encounter with Yancey, seeing no alternative, but he did not appear for supper, nor had he come home by the time she got Jonathan ready for bed.

"Ye can read tonight," Ann said, handing him their mother's Bible. She had opened it to Psalm 61, which had been one of her mother's favorites, and Jonathan remembered it, as well.

"Hear my cry, O God; attend unto my prayer. From the end of the earth will I cry unto thee, when my heart is over . . ." He stopped, and Ann supplied the rest of the word. " . . . whelmed." He continued. "Lead me to the rock that is higher than I. For thou hast been a shelter for me, and a strong tower from the enemy." He stopped reading and looked at Ann. "Ann, do ye really think we'll ever see Father again?"

"Of course we will," she assured him, although far from certain of it herself.

"Mr. Craighead said we should ask God to help us," he said. "But I wish there was something else we could do to find out where he is."

"So do I," Ann replied, "and maybe soon there will be. In the meantime, we must try to be brave, as Father would want us to be."

"I'm glad ye are here," Jonathan murmured when Ann kissed him goodnight after they had prayed together for their father.

Some time in the night Ann awoke, aware of the distant rumble of thunder and oppressive heat in the room. She got up, the corn husk mattress rattling beneath her, and crept to the window for air. So low at first that she thought she had imagined it, she heard a voice calling her name. Thunder muttered again, and sheet lightning briefly illuminated the landscape. She saw no one outside her window, but quickly lifted her robe from its hook and left the room. She wound her way quietly to the kitchen door and looked out, straining to see into the darkness. Ann had just decided it was her imagination when a form slipped from the shadows, and with a swift motion, grabbed her, covered her mouth, and half-led, half-dragged her out of the house toward a seldom-used shed across from the rear yard.

She wriggled desperately trying to see her captor's face, until he spoke. And then there was no longer any doubt who he was.

CHAPTER 13

"I HOPE I HAVEN'T HURT YOU," John Andrews said, taking his hand from her mouth, "but I feared you might wake the household."

"What on earth are ye doing here in Lancaster in the middle of the night?" she asked as they entered the shed. Lightning flashed again, and thunder roared on its heels as the storm approached.

"I had a bit of trouble over a debt and had to leave Philadelphia," he said.

"And ye are ashamed to face your father?"

"There is more to it than that," he said, and in the flash of a brilliant streak of lightning, Ann could see the drawn, defeated look on his face. In a flat tone, he continued his story. "There's no need to go into the details, but what it amounts to is that a certain gentleman wanted me to pay a debt I owed him. When I could not get the money immediately, he placed me in the position of having to defend my honor against him. It did not go well."

"Ye mean ye fought a duel?" Ann asked, astounded. In Ireland, the men of the McKay's acquaintance used their fists to settle their arguments, leaving duelling pistols or swords to the landed gentry. "Isn't that against the law?"

"Yes, and so is thievery," John said, "but goods are stolen and duels are fought, all the same." He sank to the dirt floor of the shed and rested his head against a pile of lumber. As the first raindrops peppered down, rattling the tin roof, he put his head on his drawn-up knees and made a sound very much like a sob.

"Ye say the duel did not go well—what do ye mean? Are ye hurt?"

His reply was lost in the drumming of the rain, and Ann moved closer and knelt beside him. "I couldna' hear ye. Are ye hurt?"

"Not as much as my opponent," he said bitterly. "I am told he may be mortally wounded."

Shocked, Ann drew a deep breath. It was difficult to believe that John Andrews, so light-hearted and pleasure-loving, could actually have caused someone's death. "But ye—are ye in pain?" she asked, and he nodded assent.

"We used his weapons, since I had none—a brace of matched derringers. We must have fired at the same instant, because I heard only the report of my own pistol. I felt a stinging in my left side, but I still stood. He lay on the ground and didn't move. My seconds dragged me away to an inn, and when I saw the blood on my shirt, I realized that his charge must have grazed my side."

"Then how were ye able to ride all this way?" Ann asked, recalling the hardships of the journey from Philadelphia. "Ye must be half-dead."

"One of my seconds is a surgeon's apprentice, and he bound the wound well enough so I didn't lose much blood. But then my opponent's man said he thought the other was dying. Under that condition, I had no choice but to leave."

"What will ye do now?" Ann asked. "Your father is certain to find out."

"True, but I prefer to keep it hidden as long as I can. My father can be a very hard man when he chooses, and I have no desire to put my mother in the position of harboring a fugitive."

"Surely no one will come all the way from Philadelphia after ye, will they?"

"That is not the way things are done in the Colony. There will be a public announcement posted in town and run in the *Gazette* to the effect that one John Andrews is afoul of the law, and that any citizen who apprehends him can be assured of a reward. Once that comes out, I will be in great danger, because there are those who make a handsome living from chasing runaway slaves and indentured servants—and criminals. I had to ride hard to put distance between me and the newspaper."

"Ye still have not said what ye aim to do."

"I will," he promised, "but first do you think you could find some food? I've not eaten all day."

"Of course!" she said, turning for the door. "I should have realized your need."

In the kitchen Ann found bread and a pastry, filled with apples and spices in the German way, and added cheese and mutton and buttermilk from the cooling slab in the cellar. The rain had subsided to a soft drizzle as she returned to the shed, her arms so full that she had to walk slowly.

John sat where she had left him, so still that at first she feared that he had fainted. "Here," she said, spreading an apron to serve as a tablecloth. "I was afraid to draw water, the well-chain rattles so, but I found a half-crock of buttermilk."

When he had eaten most of the food, she spoke again. "Now, tell me what ye plan to do."

"There isn't much I can do, except push on to the new lands until this business is forgotten."

"When do ye think ye can go back?"

"Not for months, maybe even years. In the meantime, I'll be fairly safe on the frontier."

"But how will ye live?" Reading law was a poor preparation for breaking land, she knew.

"I can't tell Father what happened, and I can't ask him for help, but I know where he keeps the stores he sells to traders, and I know how to get to them."

His words called to mind another trader. "Do ye know a man named Paul Yancey?"

"A rough fellow, fond of rum, as I recall. Why do you ask?"

Ann told John of her encounter with the man. "I was going to ask your father to help me trace the truth of his story, but he was not at supper."

"Do you know if he came home at all tonight?" John asked.

"No, I don't. Your mother retired to her room directly after supper, and Jonathan and I were in ours before full dark. He was not home by then. Is it important?" she asked, sensing his anxiety.

"It could be," he replied, and hesitated. "Ann, I will tell you something about my father, but it must be held in the strictest confidence. You must promise that you will never mention it to anyone else."

"Ye should not be telling me anything like that," Ann said uneasily.

"Ordinarily I wouldn't, but you should know that my father is not exactly what he seems to be." He paused, and for a moment the only sound in the shed was the rain dripping from the roof. "I found out by accident several years ago that Father is engaged in illegal trade with the French. I understand how it began, and I have reason to believe that he would like to end it now, but he has been threatened with financial ruin if he does not continue to do as they wish. Yancey is one of the go-betweens in the trade, and there is no love lost between them."

Ann remembered Yancey's words—"James Andrews is crooked as a serpent"—words she had discounted as the rantings of a drunken man. Although she knew that Mr. Andrews hoped to accumulate as much wealth as he could, she had never seen him behave in an unseemly way, and told John so.

"Do you think Yancey means to do your father harm?" she added.

"Not as long as Father is useful to him. But Yancey has no loyalty to anyone, and if he thought there was a profit in it, he would sell his very soul."

"I don't fully trust Yancey myself," Ann said, "but he has information about where my father might be, and at this point I am almost ready to believe him."

"I think you should avoid the man," John said bluntly. "It is my guess that he and Father are moving stores tonight in secret. They smuggle cargo by water every few months."

"How will ye get your stores, then, if your father is at the warehouse tonight?"

"I'll have to wait until he has finished, that's all. Now, let's consider what you should do."

"What I should do?" Ann echoed, surprised. "I should think that ye'd be too concerned with your own problems to bother yourself with mine."

"Maybe we can help each other," John said. "You want to find your father, and with the word soon out that there is a price on my head, I need to go to the frontier. The authorities will be looking out for a man alone, not for a couple. With some work on changing our appearances, I think we could escape notice. Suppose you received a letter from your father, telling you to join him," he said slowly, "and saying that Jonathan should stay here, because of his health."

"But Father would never ask me to travel alone," Ann protested, "and I wouldn't leave Jonathan here by himself, anyway."

"If he went with us, there would be greater danger

131

of detection," John pointed out. "He could easily give us away by saying the wrong thing."

How well she knew her brother's tendency to speak when he should be silent, Ann thought. "I couldn't just go off supposedly on my own, anyway," Ann said aloud. "Your father would never permit it."

"I'll grant you that," John agreed. "There must be some way that we can invent an escort for you."

"We could invent any number of things, but I have no way to travel anywhere at the moment."

"Do you ride?" he asked.

"When I was a child I would sometimes sneak into the lord's pasture and ride bareback, but I've never sat a saddle. Anyway, where would I get a mount? I have very little money."

John sighed. "It's very late, and I'm almost past thinking. I'll sleep here in the shed tonight, and stay behind this lumber during the day. As soon as you can get away tomorrow, bring me some food. By then I should have worked out a plan for us."

"Will ye be all right? Shouldn't your wound be attended?"

"It doesn't hurt so much, now that I'm off that jolting excuse of a horse—and, in any case, I can't afford to let anyone know I am in town."

"What did ye do with the horse?" Ann asked.

"I left him at the Watters stable, with no one the wiser. I can get him back, and a mount for you as well, if need be."

"Are ye sure ye won't come inside?" Ann asked. "It seems to me that your parents would want to help ye."

"They must not know about this," John said emphatically. "Can I count on you to keep my secret, sweet Ann?"

It was the first time that night that he had said anything personal to her, and for a moment he almost sounded like the John Andrews she had known before. But then his voice grew more serious, and he said "My life is in your hands." He sounded so desperate that she felt she had no choice.

"I will not tell your parents," she promised, "and I'll bring food to ye tomorrow when I can."

Back in her room, Ann lay still a long time, pondering her and John's predicaments. A fragment of Scripture came into her mind, and she repeated it several times . . . "In all thy ways acknowledge Him, and He shall direct thy path." She desperately needed direction, but as light returned to her room, Ann was no nearer to knowing what she should do than she had been before.

Called away on a business matter . . . that was Mrs. Andrews' explanation for her husband's absence from the breakfast table the next morning.

"And what ails you this morning?" Mrs. Andrews asked, when Ann made little response to her declarations. "Are you coming down with something? I'll not have you get sick on me! Agnes can prepare a posset—"

"No," Ann interrupted, attempting a smile. "I'm quite well, thank ye. It's just that the storm kept me awake, and I'm a bit tired."

"Well, I still say you look unwell," Mrs. Andrews declared, returning her attention to her food, "and I think you should stay in the house today and not go gadding about in the heat as you seem to have formed the unwise habit of doing."

When Ann went to the kitchen to fetch Mrs. Andrews a second cup of tea, Agnes commented on the missing food. "I put it away myself, from supper."

"I'm afraid I ate it," Ann said, her eyes downcast.

"Yer needed a bit o'flesh on yer bones when yer come here, I'll grant," Agnes said earnestly, "but overdo it, and yer'll have trouble catching a man."

"I'll remember your advice," Ann said, smiling. Despite her rough ways and appearance, Agnes was good-hearted, and Ann knew that she would do her best to care for Jonathan if Ann were not there to look after him. But she still could not accept the idea of leaving him with the Andrews while she went to look for their father.

The morning hours seemed to crawl by. At both breakfast and dinner she had managed to sneak some bread and cheese into her pocket, and hoped that it would suffice if Agnes did not leave the kitchen and give her a chance to raid for more.

Finally Mrs. Andrews was settled for her afternoon rest, and Jonathan was off to play with his friend, leaving Ann with her first free time of the day. "I'm going to take a walk," she told Agnes, tying on her bonnet. "I won't be gone long."

Agnes looked up from the potatoes she was peeling and grunted. "'Tis a strange time o'day to be goin' out," she said. "Mind you watch where you walk."

"I will," Ann promised. "It's much cooler today, and I just want to get out of the house for a while."

"Go, then," Agnes said, resuming her work.

When Ann entered the shed John Andrews put out both his hands and took hers in greeting. In the light of day, dark shadows under his eyes and the stubble of beard covering his face changed him from the carefree young man he had been only a short time before. When he dropped her hands, Ann brought the food from her pocket. "This is all I could get today. Agnes missed what I took last night, and I had to tell her that I ate it myself."

John unwrapped the cheese. "Thank you. I didn't intend trouble for you," he said, taking a bite before continuing. "I have formulated a plan for us. It may take a few days to work it all out, but we can make a start laying the groundwork right away. You need to receive a letter from your father saying that he is near

Harris's ferry and that he wants you and your brother to join him there. At the same time, my father must receive a letter asking him to finance your trip, to be repaid on whatever terms he chooses. He will ask Father to find a trustworthy escort for you both, say a family traveling in that direction. I'll stay around here in the woods by the river until I know what arrangements have been made, then I'll ride out west alone. Somewhere along the way, I'll meet you and say that I have been sent to take you to your father, and we'll leave the west trail and go on to Shawnee Creek together. How does that sound?"

"It might work," Ann admitted, trying to follow his reasoning, "but I wouldn't feel right, asking Mr. Andrews to pay our way."

"Don't worry about that—you work very hard around here, just for your board. You've earned more than enough to finance your trip."

"But what if Jonathan recognizes you when you join us?"

"I will try to disguise my appearance, but Jonathan is old enough to obey you if you tell him he must not appear to recognize me. He might enjoy the game, if it's put to him that way."

"And the letters from Father—how will ye manage that?"

"I think you should write them. I will get the necessary materials tonight and leave them in the shed. Then I will come back tomorrow night to pick up the letters."

"How will you get them to me and your father?"

"That can be arranged—the ferry man on the Conestoga can find someone to deliver them for a few coppers, with no questions asked."

"So we could be ready to leave in a few days," Ann said, calculating the time involved."

"I should think so. Families pass through Lancaster on their way to the west every day. It shouldn't take Father long to find one that you can travel with."

135

"But suppose your father doesn't agree that we should go? Suppose he says he can't find us an escort?"

"I know that he will not welcome the news that you are leaving, but you came with the understanding that it was a temporary arrangement, and whatever else my father may be, he has always been a man of his word in a business arrangement."

"What else should the letter say?" Ann asked. She did not like deception, and felt herself stalling. "Won't everyone wonder why Father waited so long to write?"

"Not if he had just found his land when he came down with the fever and has just now recovered. You'll know how to word it. Come to the shed tonight as soon as everyone else is asleep."

It all seemed to be happening too quickly. There were too many unanswered questions, and Ann felt an uneasy fearfulness growing in her. She spoke once more. "Making all of these arrangements," Ann began haltingly, "well, I know ye'd be better off just going alone. Perhaps that's what ye'd best do."

"Do you want to find out what has happened to your father?" he asked.

"Of course. But what will we do if we can't find him? Or if we find that he is . . . " She stopped, unable to voice the possibility that had more and more haunted her in the past few weeks.

John put his hands on her shoulders and looked into her eyes. "In any case, you and Jonathan will at least have me," he assured her. "I will see to it that you are taken care of, and that's a vow."

"I don't want ye to feel obligated to us."

John spoke in a low voice. "I need your help, Ann. Can I count on you?"

She nodded. "I'll come for the paper tonight."

CHAPTER 14

JAMES ANDREWS APPEARED AT THE SUPPER TABLE. looking tired, but quite solicitous of Martha. Ann found it hard to believe that he had been regularly breaking the law for years. She had never known her father to do less than the law required, and although William McKay had never been able to lavish his family with the comforts that James Andrews provided, his integrity was his treasure. She knew that John did not hold his father in such high regard, and she felt genuinely sad that he could not.

James Andrews retired early that evening, and Ann sat up with Mrs. Andrews for some time. Finally everyone was in bed, and even though it was well before midnight, Ann decided to visit the shed and see if John had already left the writing materials for her.

He was there, waiting, when she stepped inside. He had brought several sheets of heavy paper, a quill, and a small container of India ink. "You'll have to seal the letters with candle wax. Leave them here, under this board, tomorrow night," he directed, "and then, leave a note for me here as soon as Father has received the letters and made some plans."

137

"Be careful," Ann cautioned.

"And you, too."

Ann had no scrap paper on which to practice the wording of the letters, so she thought them through before she dared commit them to paper. Afraid to work by day, she waited until Jonathan was sleeping soundly before she dipped the quill into the ink and began to write by candlelight. She held the quill at an awkward angle and formed the letters more vertically than in her usual writing, trying to imitate William's hand. She purposely crossed out a few words, and misspelled a few others in both letters, and when she had finished, she re-read them and was satisfied. It was not a perfect forgery, by any means, but close enough, she hoped, for James Andrews to accept without question.

She blew out the candle and slipped out of the room, making her way quietly to the shed. After placing the letters under the board, Ann looked out the door in all directions to be sure she had not been observed. In the light of the waxing moon, she could detect nothing. As soon as she was back in the house, she waited by a window, watching, and saw a shadow detach itself from the wall of a neighboring house. A lone figure entered the shed, emerged a moment later, and was soon swallowed up in the night shadows.

Ann sighed and got ready for bed. For better or worse, John's plan had been set into motion. She thought of praying, but she wasn't at all sure God approved of such a plan. She felt quite sure Caleb would not. In the end, all she could do was wait, and wonder where their actions would lead them.

The next day dawned heavy with clouds, and a steady rain more typical of early spring than summer, fell all morning. As Ann and Jonathan were eating their noon-day dinner with Martha Andrews, a light rap sounded on the front door, and presently Agnes came into the dining room and handed Ann a folded paper. It was so creased and soiled that at first she did not recognize it as her work.

"Is it from Father?" Jonathan asked eagerly, leaving his place at the table to stand beside her. "What does he say?"

"Yes, it is from Father," she said, her heart pounding. How could she manage such a pretense! She continued after staring at the paper for a moment. "He says he has had the fever but has recovered, and he wants us to join him."

"Where is he?" Mrs. Andrews asked.

"I don't know," Ann answered, grateful for that bit of honesty. "He says we are to come to Harris' ferry."

"Merciful heavens!" Mrs. Andrews exclaimed. "That's many days' journey from Lancaster. How does he expect a lone girl and a little boy to make a trip like that? The man must still be feverish, even to think of such a thing."

"He says that he is also writing to Mr. Andrews, and that perhaps he can arrange a way for us to go there."

"Well, it doesn't sound sensible to me," Mrs. Andrews responded. "And, anyway, what am I going to do when you leave me? I'm afraid I have become quite dependent on you, Mistress McKay."

Jonathan began dancing around the table, emitting war whoops, until Ann had to excuse herself and take him from the room. She welcomed the opportunity to leave Mrs. Andrews. John's plan seemed to be working so far. They should soon be on their way.

The other letter that Ann had written was delivered to Mr. Andrews while he was taking his noonday meal in the company of Karl Watters, owner of the livery stable.

As James told Ann that evening, Karl's brother and

his wife were planning to go to Harris' ferry quite soon, having decided to set up a grist mill in the vicinity. She and Jonathan would be able to travel with a respectable family. "Of course, they're only a few years away from the Palatine, and their English is still rather poor. That might cause you some problems."

"I could speak for them when English was needed," Ann said.

"And I know some German," Jonathan added. He had been playing with several German children and had learned quite a few words, as Agnes discovered one day when he brought home some German phrases she recognized as most unsuitable.

"Karl Watters seems to think that you could go with his brother practically free—for a keg of flour, some salt, and a bit of other provision. Do you want me to arrange it?"

"Oh, yes!" Ann exclaimed.

"We really don't want you to leave us," James Andrews said, putting a a hand on the boy's shoulder. "Your presence has been a great help to Mrs. Andrews, and she will miss you sorely."

"And I will miss her, too, and your lovely home. But we long to see our father, and we are all he has now."

"I understand," James said. "And tell your father that I am happy to do this for him in lieu of wages you might have been paid for your work."

"That is kind of ye, and I thank ye for him," Ann said.

"Shouldn't we say a prayer of thanksgiving, like Mr. Craighead did on the ship?" Jonathan asked at bedtime.

"Yes, we should," Ann murmured. How long ago it seemed since they had all bowed together in sight of their new land, grateful they had been delivered from the hazards of the voyage! But tonight, though Ann was grateful they would soon be on their way, she felt equally apprehensive about their next journey, and what they would find at the end of it.

CHAPTER 15

JAMES ANDREWS WAS AS GOOD as his word, and he came home at noon the next day to tell Ann that the Watterses had agreed to take her and Jonathan to Harris's ferry in exchange for some extra stores.

"A carpenter is making a frame to carry the millstone, and it should be ready tomorrow. Karl said they plan to leave Lancaster early the next morning."

"This is entirely too sudden for my liking," Martha Andrews complained. "Whatever am I going to do without Ann?"

"I have given the matter some thought, and I believe that I can find a suitable replacement for Miss McKay, and some help for Agnes, as well. It will necessitate a trip to Philadelphia, but if I leave tomorrow morning, I can be back in a few days with a pair of servants," James Andrews said. "How would that suit you?"

"I'm not sure," Mrs. Andrews replied. "I'll not have any with rough manners or who cannot speak decent English."

"I will look for a suitable couple who will consent to indenture," he assured her.

Ann realized he was bound to find out about his son's disgrace when he reached Philadelphia and tried to visit him. So far no copy of the *Pennsylvania Gazette* had arrived in Lancaster. Erratic in its delivery, it usually could be counted on three days after its Philadelphia publication. Surely the next issue would carry notice of John's duel.

Ann felt compassion for father and son, though she did not condone the act of duelling, nor understand how John had come by the debts that had led to it.

That afternoon Ann wrote a brief note to John, giving the date of their departure, and adding "Leave *now*." She put the unsigned note under the board in the shed.

Afraid that Jonathan's high spirits were disturbing Mrs. Andrews' rest, Ann decided that they should get out of the house for a while.

"We should let the Alexanders know we are leaving and that ye'll not be in the catechism class tomorrow," she told him, suggesting they pay a visit.

While Jonathan played with the youngest Alexander child, Jane Alexander invited Ann to take tea with her.

"I know you will be happy to join your father," she said when Ann told her their plans, "But you must know that we will be sorry to see you leave our congregation."

"Thank ye. Everyone here has been kind to us, and I am certain we shall always remember Lancaster fondly."

"Well, you must come back for a visit one of these days. Tell me, does Reverend Craighead know about your latest plan?"

"No, he doesn't." Ann realized that the Alexanders could tell him her true destination. "If ye do hear from him, tell him he can inquire for us at a place called Shawnee Creek, just south of Tolliver Station. I am not exactly sure where Father is now, but I'll leave word there in case anyone should inquire."

"Tolliver Station," Jane Alexander repeated, and looked disturbed. "Seems that I heard of some trouble there recently."

"There was news about settlers killing some Indians, and then being killed in revenge."

"On, yes, I remember now. Terrible business, that was. But out there in the new lands, you never know what any man will do, red, black or white. It's all the same. The unredeemed human heart is utterly depraved, and capable of any crime." Mrs. Alexander spoke with the calm assurance of one who had long since made peace with God.

Ann envied the woman's complete composure. "Mrs. Alexander, did ye ever have any doubts—about God or His care for ye?"

"Doubts?" she echoed. "The catechism tells us that both mind and nature reveal God's existence. His Word and Spirit work to convict man of his sin, and reveal the salvation of Christ. But you've been nurtured in the faith from childhood, Miss McKay, and you must already know those things. Reverend Craighead told us that your mother was one of the strongest Christians he has ever known."

"But I am not as strong as she was," Ann confessed, "and sometimes my faith is very weak."

"We are also taught that if we pray for more faith, it will be given to us. That is the only way any of us can be strong—in the strength of the Lord."

"Ye remind me of my mother," Ann said. "She always said that I must be strong, too, but I have ever felt weak and powerless, instead."

"I shall pray for you," Mrs. Alexander said sincerely. "But I can tell you this much—you will never be able to draw on God's strength until you have put your trust in His Son, Jesus. If you have not done that already, I pray that you will not delay further."

"I have always attended church," Ann said, "and I understand the doctrine of salvation. I just have never been certain that I have experienced it."

"The Bible teaches us that those who come to Him He will in no wise cast out. But you must take the first step, in faith, of your own free will. When you have completely yielded your life to Christ, without any doubts or reservations whatsoever, you'll know His peace. You'll feel it *here*," she said, touching her heart.

"Ye have given me much to think on," Ann said, rising to leave, "and I thank ye for your words, and your prayers as well. My brother and I will have need of them before our journey is ended."

"You're most welcome," Mrs. Alexander replied, taking one of Ann's hands in both of hers and kissing her lightly on the cheek. "I think you are closer to God than you realize. He has a plan for you if you will but seek His will."

"I will write you and Reverend Alexander when I reach my father."

"Please do, and may God protect you all."

Ann's physical journey might end soon, if she found her father. Could it be, she wondered, that like Christian, her spiritual journey was nearing its end, as well? Or did one ever reach the end of that pilgrimage in this life? In the midst of questions, one thing was certain: Jane Alexander's words would stay in her mind.

Ann spent her last day in Lancaster with Martha Andrews, finishing some sewing for her and listening to her complaints about the couple James Andrews proposed to bring home from Philadelphia. James had left early that morning, after calling Ann aside and pressing some coins into her hand.

"These are gold pieces, to be used in case of emergency," he said. "Hide them on your person and let no one know you have them. Sometimes thieves stop travelers in the forest, where they can take what is easy to get and disappear into the trees. With the millstone, your party will move slowly, and you must stay alert. Don't let Jonathan out of your sight.''

"Thank ye, and I'll remember your advice. But I can't take the money. Ye've been more than generous already.''

"It's no more than you deserve, and I insist that you take it,'' he said firmly, and turned away.

So Ann had made a pouch for the coins and tied it to the top of her petticoat. By evening, everything had been done that could be to prepare for their journey, and in a few hours, they would be on their way.

It was still light and Ann had just listened to Jonathan's prayers when she heard loud voices, one of them Agnes', apparently from the kitchen. Then they faded, and when Ann walked out into the rear garden, she saw Agnes coming back toward the house—and the trader Yancey, retreating down the alleyway.

"That man Yancey,'' Agnes sputtered, her face more than usually red. "A lower dog ne'er walked.''

"What did he want?''

"Well, first he asked to see Mr. Andrews, an' when I tol' him he wasn't home, he said he'd see *yer* instead. The very idea! Yer can b'lieve that I sent him off, and that in a hurry.''

"Did he say what his business was?'' Ann asked uneasily.

"He said he had news about Master John, then he said to tell yer he was leavin' soon as he talked to Mr. Andrews, as if yer'd care a pin what the likes o' him did.''

"How strange,'' Ann said. "What do ye suppose he meant about John?''

"Prob'ly just an excuse to get in the door,'' Agnes said. "Well, the master'll be in Philadelphia soon enough, and can get the straight of it from John himself. Likely he's run up more debts for his father to pay."

"I suppose that it takes a great deal of money to live in a city like Philadelphia," Ann offered.

"Humph!" Agnes grunted. "That it may do, but Master John has his own reasons for needin' money."

"What do ye mean?" Ann asked.

"I mean that he has the gentleman's fondness for gamin' without much talent for winnin'."

"John gambles? Is that why he is in debt?"

Agnes laughed. "Lor' me, yes, he gambles regular, he does. One o' these days he'll get it out of his system, mayhap, but in the meantime, he's cost his father a pretty penny."

"I am sorry to hear it," Ann said, disturbed. It had never occurred to her that John's debts were related to gambling—the greatest of all vices, according to William McKay.

"Well, yer have enough to think on, what wi' yer trip and seein' yer Pa again. As I tol' yer before, Master John is a charmer. He'll come out on his feet, just like a cat dropped out of a tree."

As soon as she could, Ann crept back out to the shed and lifted the board where she had hidden her note. It was gone, and so, she presumed, was John.

Later, sleep proved elusive. Ann's mind kept turning over Agnes' words, and those of Jane Alexander. Since their journey was founded on deception, she felt it would almost be blasphemous to ask God to bless it. When at last she slept her dreams were of Caleb. Although she could see him clearly, she could not speak to him and tell him where she was.

CHAPTER 16

AGNES, UP BEFORE HER ACCUSTOMED HOUR, had prepared a lavish farewell breakfast of fried ham, eggs, thin buckwheat cakes cooked on an iron griddle, and a quantity of honey.

"Heaven knows when yer'll see another decent meal," Agnes said when Ann protested at the amount of food they were served. "Yer may as well eat hearty one more time."

"We'll miss your cooking," Ann said. "I really think it saved Jonathan's life."

Agnes looked fondly at the boy and sighed. "Well, he does look better'n what he did when yer come here. And maybe travelin' with the Dutch, yer'll be well-fed. They do like their victuals."

"Food is the least of my concerns now," Ann confided after her brother left the table. "Last night Jonathan put Indians and pirates in his prayers, asking to be protected from both. There could be some renegade Indians about, and Mr. Andrews said something about watching out for thieves. I just hope that Mr. Watters will be able to defend us if need be."

"If he's aught like his brother Karl, he will be," Agnes assured her. "They're strong men, and brave as they come. Now let me help yer get yer belongings outside afore y'er come for."

Ann took a breakfast tray in to Mrs. Andrews. "I thought ye might like to bide in bed awhile longer this morning," she said, setting the tray on a bedside table.

Mrs. Andrews' expression was unusually dour. "Ah, Mistress Ann, it is a sad day for this household. Even now, I wish you would change your mind about rushing off into the wilderness and stay here with us."

"I must go to my father," Ann said. "Soon Mr. Andrews will be bringing ye a new companion, and some help for Agnes, as well. That is something ye can look forward to. And just think how peaceful it will be around the house without Jonathan's noise."

"It will be more lonely than peaceful," she declared sadly. "With my children so far away, this has been a desolate house. For at least a little while, you and Jonathan brought some life into it. I do not begrudge your father the right to have you back, but I wish it did not have to be this soon. And, should anything go amiss with him, I hope you will remember that you will always have a home with us."

It was possibly Martha Andrews' longest and kindest speech ever, and knowing that the woman would soon hear the bad news about John, Ann felt a rush of pity for her. Bending over, she kissed her cheek. "Thank ye for taking us in when we needed a home," she said. "Jonathan and I may never see ye again, but we'll never forget ye for that."

Agnes summoned her, and Ann went outside to find the livery man standing in front of the house, holding the reins of a laden pack-horse.

"'Mornin', Mistress," he said in thickly-accented English. "Mine brother is vaiting for you and der boy. With a final embrace for Agnes, Ann and Jonathan

149

followed Karl Watters to the edge of Lancaster, where his brother awaited them.

Klaus Watters was about thirty, a huge man, standing over six feet tall and well-muscled, obviously a valuable ally in a fight. His wife Maria made up in girth what she lacked in height. She wore her glossy black hair in braids close to her head, and her deep-set eyes were dark and alert. Her plump, rosy cheeks and generous mouth, which turned up at the corners, gave her a look of perpetual amusement. Both husband and wife greeted Ann and Jonathan warmly as Karl introduced them.

"Now ve start," Klaus said, heaving Ann's trunk effortlessly onto the cart containing the Watters' household goods. A yoke of oxen pulled the cart, a larger and heavier version of the one that had brought the McKays to Lancaster.

Another yoke of oxen was attached to a triangular wooden frame that held the millstone that would assure the Watters' livelihood at the end of their journey. This contraption was not fitted with wheels, but was designed so that only one small point of the triangular frame touched the ground. Ann had never seen anything like it, but as they got underway, she saw that it moved the heavy stone quite efficiently. In addition to the pack horse Karl Watters had brought to the Andrews' house, two other pack horses made up the procession, and one riding horse was tied to the back of the cart.

"Der boy can sit der horse if he vants," Karl Watters told her as he bade them farewell. "It is a gift to him from James Andrews."

"Oh! Please thank him for us." Ann was surprised at the gift, but accepted it, thinking they might need a horse when John joined them.

The sun was well up and at their backs, promising a hot and dry day, when the little caravan finally got underway. Klaus led the team that pulled the millstone. Ann and Jonathan walked along beside Maria, who directed the team pulling the cart by voice commands and a hand on the yoke when necessary.

The terrain was, at first, identical to that which they had encountered as they came to Lancaster from Philadelphia. On the road ahead of them, cultivated land alternated with patches of dark woods; the trees on either side of the trail formed an overhead canopy that provided a welcome relief from the heat of the sun.

At their first rest stop, with several hours' travel behind them, Klaus Watters unfolded a crude parchment map of the area, marked with streams and names in a few places. At the far left-hand margin, designated with an X, was Harris's ferry. Other drawings indicated the location of springs and likely camping places. Although she tried to make out all of the names, Ann did not see either Tolliver Station or Shawnee Creek, but she did note the location of Conewago Creek, the stream that the trader Yancey had mentioned. It appeared about halfway between Harris' ferry and Lancaster. She wondered how many days away it was.

By late afternoon of the first day's journey, the land began to change, from flat to gently rolling to steep, winding upward seemingly forever. Twilight deepened into night, and when Ann had despaired of ever reaching the summit, they rounded one last turn in the trail and came upon open ground. Ashes of old campfires, evidence that others had used this place before them, dotted the broad meadow.

In the light of the campfire, with Maria moving about preparing their evening meal, Jonathan crept close to his sister and put his head in her lap. He was tired, as was she, but he was still excited about their trip. "Do ye think that Father camped here, too?" he asked.

"'Tis likely. How do ye feel?"

"Weary of walking," he admitted, "and I'd like to ride tomorrow, if ye'll let me."

"Sitting in a saddle may not be as comfortable as ye think, but ye can try," Ann said. When John came for them, she would have to ride, too, and she would like to practice a bit first. As they settled down to sleep that night, she wondered where John was, and if he, too, had camped in this meadow.

Ann found the Watterses surprisingly easy to understand. Like most of the German settlers in those parts, they spoke only German at home, in their churches, and with their fellow countrymen, but had learned enough English to get by in most ordinary situations. His wife, who seemed naturally reticent, wept as she haltingly told Ann of their voyage from Rotterdam, through the North Sea and then across the Atlantic, on which two of their children had died. Since coming to Lancaster, another child had been taken by the fever, and their last son had drowned early that summer in the mill pond.

"So ve go away from der place where is trouble," Maria explained.

Ann told Maria of losing her mother on the voyage over, and a special bond of understanding was forged between them.

That bond was strengthened by prayers and Bible-reading. The Watterses' massive Bible, printed in heavy Gothic lettering, fascinated Jonathan; their prayers, spoken in German, touched Ann. She did not understand their guttural tongue, but their invocation, their God, their faith was universal. Prayers and praise really did rise to heaven from every tongue. In that wild land, still largely untouched by the hand of man, Ann felt the assurance of God's presence.

On the third day of the journey, their slow but steady progress was halted by a downpour that forced them to seek shelter under the cart. Ann watched as Klaus traced their route on the map, pointing out a small square that appeared to be near their present location. "Ve stop by here next," he told them. "Is trading post. Ve sleep dere."

"In a real bed?" Jonathan asked. The novelty of sleeping out-of-doors had worn off, and the monotony of the journey was dampening his spirits.

"Vell, in a house mit a roof and walls," Klaus replied, hiding a smile.

"How far are we from here?" Ann asked, pointing to a wavy line labeled "Conewago Cr."

"Mabby vun day. Vy do you ask?"

"My father knows someone who lives near there." She knew she should begin to prepare the way for John's appearance.

"Mabby ve see him, den," Klaus said, folding the map and replacing it inside his shirt.

With some hours of daylight still remaining after the rain ceased, they were able to reach the trading post.

Sturdily built of notched logs, and far smaller than a regular inn, the dwelling provided shelter from the elements for several travelers. The wiry owner proudly told them his name was Walters and that his was the first permanent dwelling to be built west of Lancaster.

Ann asked him if he had seen William McKay.

"Well, now, people stop here almost every day," he told her. "Some days I've had as many as four families sleeping in the cabin and more camped out in the shed. I seldom recall a name."

"What about a minister, a man about thirty, riding alone with one pack horse? He could have passed this way within the past ten days."

"There's been no one claiming to be a minister, though several would fit that description otherwise. Last night it was a young man with a yellow beard, who took supper with us like he hadn't et in a month, then rode off like a spook was after him when one of John Penn's men rode in from Philadelphia on a

153

survey run. Most would have stayed to hear the latest news of the city, but not that one!" he added.

Seeing that the Watterses and Jonathan were occupied with livestock, she took the opportunity to inquire about Tolliver Station.

"It's not on the western trail," he said. "About three hours due west of here, you'll come to a branch. If you bear north and to the west, you'll be going toward Harris's ferry. Go south along Conewago Creek, and you'll come to Tolliver Station directly. There was some trouble there lately. Some fool hot-headed Irish broke a treaty that was scarce a year old, and now nobody is sure what the Shawnee will do."

Ann wanted to ask him more questions, but he was needed outside, and left her to think on his words. Ann was almost certain that the man who had fled from the post the night before was John. He had probably been watching them from the woods for several days, and when he learned of the Philadelphia surveyor's arrival, feared he would be recognized from the latest fugitive notices. He must be somewhere ahead of them, waiting.

When Walters came back into the cabin, Ann asked if he had any newspapers, and after some rummaging, he produced the tattered remains of a *Pennsylvania Gazette*.

"What happens in the city doesn't mean much out here," he said, and Ann took comfort in his indifference.

Klaus Watters was already outside, hitching the oxen to the cart when Ann awoke at sunrise, and after a breakfast of corn meal mush, they got underway.

The trail was overgrown and travel was slow. They climbed or descended one small ridge after another until late afternoon. When they finally reached a valley clearing, Ann thought she could make out a fork in the trail ahead, just before it disappeared into the beginnings of yet another pine-covered ridge. Threading through the valley was a flow of ankle-deep water. The sides of the creek bed were steep and rocky. Klaus halted the oxen and took out his map.

"Conewago Creek," he said, showing Ann the mark.

"Ve must cross now," Klaus added, scanning the sky. Rolling thunder and rising wind threatened a storm, and Ann realized, as the first few sprinkles fell around her, that a heavy rainfall could fill the stream, making the crossing with the huge mill wheel almost impossible.

Klaus would lead the pack horses across first, followed by Ann leading the riding horse, with Jonathan astride. Then Klaus would return to bring the cart and the millstone across with his wife's help. It was a plan they had utilized in fording several small streams the day before, and it had worked perfectly each time.

However, by the time they reached the creek and were positioned for the crossing, heavy rain was falling, and even as Ann took her first step down the side of the creek bank, the stream was already beginning to rise. "Hang on," she called to Jonathan, her words snatched away in the din of the thunder and the roar of the rain.

Ahead, she could barely see the pack horses as they picked their way through a curtain of rain. So much lightning flashed around them that it was difficult to distinguish any separate strokes. The horse Ann was guiding laid back his ears and tossed his head nervously, but Ann pulled on the lead, and then the bridle itself, forcing the animal on. An eternity later Klaus held out his hand to help Ann climb up the slippery bank on the other side. He lifted Jonathan from the horse's back.

"Keep down!" he yelled as lightning struck a pine tree a hundred yards away, flaring briefly like a fiery torch until the rain quenched it. Ann sank to her knees, sheltering Jonathan as well as she could while holding onto the horse's reins.

Klaus quickly waded back to the opposite shore, through water that had risen almost to his knees. Ann strained forward, trying to see through the driving rain.

Surely he won't try to cross in this downpour! From bank to bank, the distance was perhaps fifty feet, but with the stream filling rapidly from run-off coming down the ridges, it had become a swift-flowing torrent.

As Ann watched, the oxen moved forward, prodded by Klaus into the turbulent waters. The cart lurched sideways as it caught the current, and Ann held her breath as Klaus struggled forward. She was certain with his every step that all would be swept away, yet with his sheer size and strength, and the dogged determination to keep going, Klaus was inching his way toward them.

A shout sounded above the wind, and Ann saw a horseman hesitate only a moment before urging his mount forward into the water. It struggled for a foothold, then spurred on by his rider, the animal reached midstream. The rider steadied the cart that the current was threatening to wrench away, and helped bring it safely to the edge of the bank. That reached, he dismounted and waded into the water to help Klaus push the cart onto the land.

The rescuer was completely enveloped in a dark cloak, with a broad-brimmed hat obscuring his features. But as he bent over the rear of the cart, Ann glimpsed a yellow beard. *John Andrews!*

"My vife is on the other side," Klaus shouted as the cart came to a stop.

"I'll ride over for her," the man offered, and was gone before Klaus could say more. Once on the other side he lifted Maria up behind him. As he urged his horse back into the water, Maria's long skirts billowed out, becoming thoroughly soaked. In a few moments she stood huddled by Klaus, shaken but safe.

"I never saw vater rise so fast," Klaus declared, "or rain stop so suddenly." Droplets of water falling freely from leaves of the surrounding trees were the only evidence of the downpour.

"Vat about our stone?" Maria asked anxiously.

"Ve get it later," Klaus said. "Praise God ve have not all drowned. You come at a needful time," he added, addressing the horseman.

"I'm glad I could be of help. I am looking for Mistress Ann McKay and her brother. Might they be with your party?"

CHAPTER 17

AND WHO MIGHT you be?'' Klaus asked.

John had managed to disguise his voice in such a way that, with his hat pulled down over his face and cloak turned up, his own mother could not have recognized him.

''A friend of William McKay's, sent to fetch his son and daughter to him. My name is Jeffrey Lewis.''

Klaus looked at John, puzzled. ''Mr. James Andrews asked us to take them to Harris's ferry,'' he said.

''And that is where Mr. McKay was at one time,'' John replied easily. ''He has now removed to land south of Tolliver Station, and has asked me to take his children there.''

''I don't know,'' Klaus said doubtfully. ''I vas told they went to der ferry with us.''

John reached inside his cloak, brought out a scrap of paper, and handed it to Klaus. ''This is a note from Mr. McKay. He heard from a trader that Mr. Andrews had engaged a German miller to bring the children to him, and he thought to make it easier on them to come directly, rather than to go out of their way, since he is no longer at the ferry."

Klaus scowled at the words on the paper, and Ann guessed that he could not make them out. "Vell, I don't know," he said again, scratching his chin thoughtfully. He handed the note to Ann, and she looked at it carefully.

"This man is my father's friend," Ann said. "This note says that he has changed his plans, and we are to go with Mr. Lewis."

"I don't understand vy Mr. McKay did not come himself, den," Klaus said.

"He has had a fever," Ann put in quickly. "That is why he didn't come for us before. He probably thought he shouldn't travel any more than necessary, for fear of a relapse."

"Yes, that's right," John agreed. "He wanted to come himself, but I persuaded him to let me come in his place."

"If that is vat you must do, then I think that ve should all go," Klaus said.

"Oh, no!" John exclaimed, then added quickly, "The trail to the Station is steep, and with your heavy load, it would be far too difficult. Mr. McKay will appreciate your concern, but I will see to it that they reach him safely, and you can be on your way with an easy mind."

"Well, first I must have my stone," Klaus said, looking back across the creek where the oxen waited patiently. "Soon comes dark, and ve must bring it over while ve can still see."

"I think it is safe to bring it across," John said. "The current is not so strong now."

"Ve get it, den," Klaus said, and the men waded into the creek.

Jonathan remained quiet for a moment after they left, then looked steadily at Ann. "Why is John Andrews calling himself something else? And did he really come from Father?"

Ann glanced at Maria, but she was busy untying the cover on the cart, and apparently had not heard him. "There are reasons, but I can't tell ye all about it now. Just trust me when I say that John is going to make every effort to get us to Father as soon as he can. In the meantime, we must pretend that we do not know who he really is until we are away from the Watterses. It will be like a game. Can ye do that for me?"

The urgency in her voice must have communicated to him, for he nodded and said nothing as Klaus and John returned with the millstone.

"Ve must have a fire and dry out, ja?" Klaus said, seeing that Jonathan was beginning to shake with cold.

"I'll gather some wood," Ann volunteered. As she walked away, she heard John tell Klaus they would camp there that evening, and start for Tolliver Station at dawn.

"We should be there by supper time tomorrow," he was saying in his strange new voice.

Sometime in the night, when everyone else slept, Ann crept away from the campfire and walked into the forest. Her doubts about the plan had melded into a leaden feeling of sinfulness inside her. She could no longer bear the weight of it. She remembered the words of her minister's wife, that it was never too late to pray, to ask Jesus for help. So now, even though she was coming to Him out of desperation, unsure of her future, and her bridges burned behind her, she had to believe that He would not reject her. She had tried making it on her own, and was weary with the effort. It was time she let Him guide her life.

Kneeling in the damp pine straw, she acknowledged that she had done wrong, and she asked for forgiveness. For the first time, she committed her entire being to Christ, and almost immediately, she felt a strange warmth in the chill, wet forest.

Direct me, O Lord, she prayed. *Show me what I must do.*

Sodden blankets and the fog that wrapped around them like damp cotton, caused the entire party to awaken the next morning stiff and miserable.

Jonathan was listless and ate little of the hot mush Maria prepared for them. Ann prayed that she had not been the cause of bringing illness to her brother.

"We have enjoyed traveling with ye both," Ann said sincerely, after Klaus secured their luggage onto the pack horse.

"You must come to see us at der ferry," Maria said. "Maybe your father will have grain to grind, ja?"

"I hope so," Ann replied, embracing Maria. In their short time together, she had become quite fond of this calm, good-natured woman.

"Are you sure this is vot you should do?" Klaus asked in a low voice as he lifted Jonathan onto the saddle.

"Yes, it will be all right," Ann said, trying to reassure him.

"Dot man—there is something I don't like."

"I feel we are under God's care," Ann said with new conviction. "He will work things out for us." With a final wave to the Watterses, Ann and Jonathan walked with John toward the fork in the trail that would take them to Tolliver Station.

The fog persisted well up into the morning, muffling all sounds and lending an eerie stillness to the landscape. Ann looked up toward the tree tops, obscured by the mist. That was the way she had been living, she thought, with the truth hidden away in the mist of doubt she had created for herself. But even though the fog was all around her, she felt a new clearness of vision that not even the chill dampness could diminish.

They journeyed for some time in silence, and it was John who finally spoke. "I wasn't sure that man was going to let you come with me."

"Klaus Watters is a good man," Ann replied. "He only wanted to protect us from harm and do what he saw as his duty. I am sorry that I lied to him."

Lowering his voice, John moved closer. "You should watch what you say," he warned. "Jonathan can hear you."

Ann looked at Jonathan, whose eyes were regarding her steadily. He looked frightened, and Ann patted his leg and smiled reassuringly before she returned her attention to John.

"He knows who you are. He recognized you immediately, as I feared he would. I have promised to explain the situation to him later, and I will. But for my part, I regret that I ever agreed to your plan, and the sooner the truth comes out, the better it will be."

"I told you in Lancaster that I wanted to help you," John said, dropping his new accent. "If your father can be found, I'll leave you and Jonathan with him and you'll never be bothered with me again, if that is what you want."

"And if he isn't there?"

"Then we will find him, or find out what happened to him, one way or the other. I promised that I would take care of you, and I will."

"I think it best that we just get on to Tolliver Station and say no more for the present."

"If that is what you want," John replied stiffly. "But I don't see why you are so angry now."

"I am more angry with myself than with ye," Ann said, her tone softening. "I will try to explain it to ye when I have sorted it out a little better for myself."

And so they walked on, following the creek along a trail over several ridges. The trader Yancey had told Ann that some settlers had been killed near Tolliver Station, and then that many had died from the fever on Shawnee Creek, a day's journey past the Station. He had not told her how isolated the area was, or how devoid of any evidence of human life it seemed to be.

By the time they stopped at mid-day, the fog had finally dissipated; the remnants were a mere wispy wreath about the tops of the tallest trees along the ridge. The Watterses had given them more than ample provisions for several meals, but since they had no cooking utensils, they ate some cheese and picked blackberries from the prickly bushes that grew in abundance along the trail. When they were underway again, and had descended the next ridge, they found themselves in another narrow valley, a spidery criss-crossing of paths giving first evidence that others had traveled there before them.

"The trader said the stream led south to Tolliver Station," Ann said as John seemed to be considering which of the paths they should follow.

As they continued by the stream, the path widened somewhat, but there was no sign of life anywhere along it. Finally, when Ann had almost given up thinking they would find it, they came to a cleared area where three cabins stood close together. There could be no doubt that they had finally reached Tolliver's Station.

A yellow dog sleeping in the sun roused at their approach. His frantic barking summoned a man in a fringed buckskin shirt from the rear of the central cabin. Even though his grizzled hair and beard gave him a rather fierce expression and his voice sounded harsh and rusty, as if he lacked many opportunities to use it, his welcome was warm.

"Is your name Tolliver?" John asked.

"This place is known as Tolliver Station, but the Tollivers moved on south some time back. My name's Lemuel Smith."

John again introduced himself as Jeffrey Lewis, and explained that they were looking for William McKay.

"Do ye know aught of him?" Ann asked.

"Maybe, though not by name. A few weeks back, a lone man was found on the Shawnee Creek trail, sick with the fever. The Stones took him in, but what's happened to him since, I ain't heard."

"How far is that from here? Could we get there today?"

Smith scanned the sky, mentally measuring the angle of the sun's rays, and shook his head. "It's doubtful, since you don't know the lay of the land. You'd best bide here tonight and start out fresh in the morning. I'll be right glad o' the company," he added, seeing that Ann looked disappointed.

"The boy is tired," John said, "and we could all use a good rest. I think we should stay here."

"I suppose you are right," Ann said reluctantly, torn between her impatience to continue their quest and concern for her brother's welfare.

"You'll feel better after a good feed," Mr. Smith declared, and when Ann shared their stores with him, he put their food with some game he had just brought in, and produced a pungent stew.

"Are there many settlers in the valley?" Ann asked. "It seemed so deserted along the trail from Conewago Creek."

"There's more people in this valley than you'd think, and more coming in all the time. They don't all walk in, though. Lots come up the Susquehanna. Some are goin' south, too, down into the Virginny lands, particularly the Irish. I've been here nigh on to three years, and I've seen more folks in the last two months than all the rest of the time put together. Why there's so many families coming into the valley now, a blacksmith's set up at Shawnee Creek, and we even have a preacher once a month."

"A preacher?" Ann repeated, her heart leaping at the words. "Do ye happen to recall his name?"

Mr. Smith frowned and scratched his head. "A tall

fellow, rides a blaze horse. I b'lieve his name is Grayson, but I ain't for sure on it. He'll be around again in a week or so."

So it wasn't Caleb. Ann chided herself for daring to hope.

"You folks must be dead tired. Mistress, there's a lean-to in the back with room for you and the boy to spread your blankets."

"I'll take him in there," John said, scooping the sleeping boy up in his arms and laying him on the blanket Mr. Smith put down.

Bone-weary herself, Ann knew she had to talk to John before she slept, and they walked outside into a brilliantly clear night in which the heavens seemed crowded with stars. Somewhere an owl called, and a dog barked in the distance. Ann sat on a upended tub beside the cabin, with John on the ground by her side.

"You have been behaving oddly these past two days," he said. "I thought you agreed that what we are doing was the only way that you could find out about your father, but now you act as if it were something you want no part in. What has happened?"

Ann took a deep breath and began speaking, earnestly hoping he would understand how she felt. "I always knew in my heart that what we are doing was wrong, but I suppose I was so concerned about Father that I ignored the warning signals. But I've had a chance to do a lot of thinking since I left Lancaster, and last night I realized that a right thing can't be accomplished in a wrong way. I can't be proud of my part in the deception, and as soon as I can, I intend to ask your parents' pardon."

"Pardon for what?" John exclaimed. "You did nothing to harm them!"

"I did much to harm them," Ann said. "I knew about your troubles, and I remained silent, thus wronging both ye and them. Ye should have shared your problems with them from the first, and I should have seen to it that ye did. Then when Agnes told me that ye were often in debt because of gambling, I realized that ye had deceived me, too, in a way, and that gave me something else to consider."

"You must hate me," John said sadly.

"No, I don't hate ye," Ann assured him. "'Tis not my place to judge any man, or what is in any man's heart. I know your family isn't church-going, but perhaps ye know that Jesus said, 'Judge not, that ye be not judged.' Last night I asked Him for forgiveness for all the wrong that I've done and put my life in His hands. I feel absolutely certain that I have been redeemed."

Ann stopped for a moment, wondering how she could possibly relay to John the peace that had enveloped her the instant that she yielded her will to Christ. In the back of her mind she knew Caleb would understand.

"My mother once told me that she was praying that I would find God's peace and claim His promises for myself. I didn't understand what she meant for a long time, but last night I was able to do it, and even if I don't find Father, I have no doubt that God will care for me. I just wish that ye could have the same assurance for yourself."

John sighed wearily. "Ah, Ann, how easy you make it all sound! Tell me, will your newly found conscience permit you to continue to travel with a sinner like me?"

"I am afraid ye don't understand a word I've said if ye think that."

"Well, don't worry. I promise I'll not burden you much longer," he said, standing. As they went back into the cabin, Ann's heart ached to see the pain and hurt in his face. As she spread her blanket beside Jonathan, she said a prayer—an action that now seemed natural—for John to find the peace she had found, and for her to accept whatever result the search for her father would bring.

The next morning they were on the trail an hour after sunrise. Mr. Smith directed them to follow the creek until they came to a path that led up a rolling hill and into a hardwood thicket. On the other side was a clearing, he said, where they could inquire about the man who had been found on the trail nearby. "Watch for three notches in the trees just before you reach the path," he added. "Those cuts show where the Stone's land begins. Turn west, and you'll be on Stone land all the way to their clearing."

John and Ann did not talk as they made their way, and Jonathan, apparently sensing the importance of this final part of their journey, was silent as well. Midmorning they entered a large cleared area. Two cabins stood there, one completed and the other being worked on by a half-dozen men.

A chorus of barking dogs greeted them as they rode into the open, and the men stopped their work to stare at them. Ann slid down from her horse and reached for Jonathan as John swung him down to her. A woman came to the doorway of the completed cabin, shading her eyes against the sun's glare. One of the young men put down a large log he was fitting into one of the walls and came over to them. When John explained their errand the man turned and, as if in answer to Ann's desperate prayer, pointed toward the woman in the cabin door.

"You need to talk to my mother, Hannah Stone," he said, indicating a sturdy woman of middle years, with even, regular features and sun-browned skin. When Ann introduced herself and explained their mission, she smiled down at Jonathan.

"So this is the boy," she said. "Your father sets a great store by you, lad."

"Ye know him, then!" Ann exclaimed. "Is he here?"

Mrs. Stone took Ann's hand in hers. "Yes, I know him, although it was just a few days ago that he was

167

able to tell me his name. My son found him on the trail, half-dead from the fever, and brought him here for me to nurse. I never thought he'd live through the day. Two babes and a husband I've seen taken by the fever, and I've had it myself, but I've never seen anyone so sick for so long who lived through it."

"Is he all right now?"

"He's alive, and that's remarkable in itself. My son had to tie him down, he was so wild at first. He'd talk about you and his boy and someone called Sarah. Then he was unconscious for weeks. It was just three days ago that he came to himself and told us his name."

"Can we see him now?" Ann asked.

"He's mighty weak yet," Mrs. Stone warned. "I think it best that you let me talk to him first. The shock of seeing you so sudden-like might do some damage."

'Of course," Ann said, and looked down at Jonathan. "Did ye hear that? Father's here, and soon we shall see him."

Jonathan began to cry, and tears filled Ann's eyes as well as they clung together, John standing silently beside them. Spontaneously Ann voiced her joy: "Thank Ye, Lord, for leading us safely here."

William, wearing a coarse but clean homespun shirt, lay on a built-in bunk along the side of the cabin wall. His features had been sharpened by the weight he had lost, and his eyes seemed sunken and lusterless. It had been some weeks since he had shaved, and the beard was strange and unfamiliar. Yet he was William McKay, there could be no doubt of that, and the way his eyes lighted when he saw his children showed that he recognized them, as well.

"How came ye to find me in this place, where I hardly know where I am, myself?" he asked when he could speak again.

"'Tis a long story," Ann began, wiping her eyes, but Jonathan interrupted her.

"We asked God to bring us to ye, and He did."

"We had some human help, too," Ann said, smiling, and called John to come inside. "Ye must meet my father."

John took William's thin hand gently. "My name is John Andrews, James Andrews' son."

"What happened to Jeffrey Lewis?" Ann asked, lowering her voice.

"He doesn't exist any more," John whispered back.

"I lost all our things, lass," William said sadly. "Everything was gone when they found me, cart, oxen, all."

"It doesn't matter. We have found ye, and that is the important thing."

After some minutes Mrs. Stone decided that her patient had need of a rest, and suggested that they leave him for a time.

"We should see to the horses," Ann told her father, "but I'll be back to sit with ye in a bit."

"Isn't it strange how this has worked out," she said a few minutes later, helping John unload her pack horse. "It's almost as if Father really did write that letter to me."

"I'm glad that you have found him," John said sincerely. "Now that you have, I'll be riding on. Jack Stone told me I could make it to Shawnee Creek tonight. From there I can raft to the Susquehanna."

"And where will that take ye?" she asked quietly.

"To Philadelphia. I hardly slept at all last night, thinking about what you said. I know you're right, and that I can't keep running away from what I did."

"Oh, I am so glad!" Impulsively Ann threw her arms around John's neck and kissed his cheek.

"I may hang, you know," he said. "Is that why you are so pleased that I am going back?" But his tone was light, and he once again sounded almost like the John Andrews she had first known.

"Of course not," she replied. "But if ye turn yourself in and plead for mercy, I very much doubt that ye'll hang."

"So do I, now that I have had time to consider the matter. Mr. Otis has his faults, but he's an excellent lawyer and a fair man, and if he won't defend me himself, he can find someone who will."

"I am sure your parents will stand by ye, as well," Ann said. "Ye just never gave them the opportunity."

The amused look faded from John's face. "That remains to be seen," he said, "and that will be the hardest thing of all to face."

"How did ye ever get started in on gambling?" Ann asked, feeling that his gambling debts were the cause of his present trouble.

"Oh, it was exciting at first, and it passed the time. I was lucky enough to keep winning for months, so I went for higher stakes, and then I began to lose. I borrowed money, thinking to make it all up, but I just got deeper into debt instead. I never intended to harm anyone by it, and I'll never gamble again, believe me."

"Good," Ann said, and smiled.

"Are you still sorry that you came with me?" he asked.

"I am not sorry to find my father, of course, and I thank ye for your part in it. But I believe if I had told your father what Yancey told me, he would have found someone to bring me here, and the result would have been the same. I meant what I said earlier—I handled the whole thing badly."

"I would like to think that perhaps you have some small regard for me," John said, regarding her steadily. "Could you love me just a little bit, sweet Ann?"

Ann was able to return his gaze. "I know now that I

love someone else. I may never see him again, but he will always be in my heart."

John dropped his eyes. "I wish, with all my heart, that things could be different between us."

"And I wish ye happiness, John," she said gently.

CHAPTER 18

HER FIRST DAYS AT STONE'S clearing were strangely bittersweet for Ann. Along with her newfound peace of mind and great joy in being with her father again, was a nagging concern about their future.

Both Hannah and Jack Stone assured Ann that she and Jonathan were welcome to stay as long as they liked, but she felt that they were disrupting the Stone household. Mrs. Stone and her son had given up their bunks to sleep on the floor of the new cabin. Hannah Stone would not hear of changing the arrangement, however, nor would she take the money that Ann offered to help with living expenses.

Hannah shook her head emphatically. "We've had a good year, and we have no need of cash money for the present. Seeing your father well and strong is all the payment we need or want."

"At least let me help ye with the household work, then," Ann said, believing it must have been more difficult for the widow than she was letting on. "I recently nursed a woman with the fever, and I know ye've not had an easy time of it with Father."

"Well, I am a bit behind on some of the outside chores," she admitted. "If you want to do a bit of spinning as you sit with your father, I've some things that need seeing to elsewhere."

Ann readily agreed, and as she busied herself about the cabin, she was pleased to note that her father seemed to be gaining strength each day. Less than a week after their arrival at Stone's clearing, William stood and took a shaky step, and they wept together with joy. Encouraged, Ann asked him if he had given any thought to what they would do when he had regained his health.

"I have thought of little else," he said cautiously, "from the time I first felt the fever coming upon me. I thought I was going to die there on the trail with none around me, and I prayed that God would look after my children. I didn't expect that He would spare me, too, and when I woke up in this place and realized that He had given me back my life, I figured it must have been for some reason. The Stones are good people, and they've a large grant that needs much work. Since his father died, Jack has had more to do than he can handle alone, and he has asked me to stay on and help him."

William paused, looking away for a moment, and then back into Ann's eyes. "Would ye think ill of me if I took Hannah Stone to wife?" he asked.

The idea that her father might marry again had never occurred to Ann. When, in her surprise, she did not immediately reply, William continued to speak. "I know ye're thinking about your mother, and the day never passes that I don't miss her, too. No woman could ever take Sarah's place. I believe Hannah understands that, being a widow herself, but we've each a need the other can fill. I should be able to help with the harvest this year, and it won't be long until Jonathan can do a full share, as well. In all, I can only think that Providence brought us to this place."

Ann left the spinning wheel to kiss her father's cheek. "I have lately felt the same," she said, "and Hannah Stone is a fine woman. I wish ye much joy together. And I think it is time that I told ye how we happened to come here."

Ann sketched the series of events that had led her to departure from Lancaster. "At the time, I believed that circumstances justified what John and I did, but soon I began to have doubts. And when I met John at Conewago Creek and heard myself lying to Klaus Watters, I knew I had done a great injustice to everyone involved. That night I asked God to forgive me, and I feel that He has. I kept thinking of Mother, and how she always told us to have faith in God's will. I had never been able to do that, because I had not given Him my life. Now I have, and I know something of what she must have felt."

"In all thy ways acknowledge him, and he shall direct thy paths," William quoted from the Bible. "My illness has made me realize how much I need to rely on Him, too. We mustn't dwell on the wrong that might have been done, but look forward to walking in the light from now on."

"I know," said Ann, "but it grieves me that I might have hurt the Andrews. I'd like them to know how I feel."

"Then write to them, and let Jack take the letters when he goes to Shawnee Creek," William suggested.

"I'll do that," Ann said, and the thought occurred to her that she should also write to the Alexanders. She wanted Jane Alexander to know that her words had borne fruit, and it could do no harm for them to know where she was, just in case Caleb might someday return to Lancaster and inquire about her.

Later that day, Ann stopped on her way to the spring for water to talk to Jack, who was smoothing logs with a broadaxe. She asked when he was planning to go to Shawnee Creek again.

"As soon as I finish building Mother's bunk—probably tomorrow. Why do you ask?"

"I want to send some letters to Lancaster, and Father suggested that ye could take them to Shawnee Creek and find someone there to send them on."

"I'll do better than that—I'll give them to a merchant on the Susquehanna, and they'll be on their way much sooner."

"Oh, I'd not want ye to go out of your way on my account," Ann protested. "That's another half-day's journey from Shawnee Creek, isn't it?"

Jack Stone nodded, then smiled. "It is, but I was intending to go there anyway, to see someone."

"Father told me that ye have a sweetheart," Ann said. "Is that where she lives?"

"Yes. She's a merchant's daughter, newly come to the river, and I've not had much time for proper courting. But now that the new cabin's up, I plan to ask for her hand."

"And do ye think she will consent?"

"If I didn't, I wouldn't be making the trip," he said. "She's a bit of a wild thing, being Irish and red-haired to boot, but I think we'll get on."

"What is her name?" Ann asked, amused at his confidence.

"Isabel Prentiss," he said, and was about to add more when Ann's delighted exclamation stopped him.

"Oh, Jack, how wonderful! Our families crossed together from Londonderry."

"So you know her, then!"

"Isabel's the only really close friend I have ever had," Ann said. "How I would like to see her again!"

"Then ride along with me," Jack invited. "Maybe you would be willing to put in a kind word for my cause."

She smiled. "I'll see what Father thinks about it."

William, too, was amazed to hear of the Prentisses, and he agreed that Ann should accompany Jack on his visit. When Jonathan heard of it, he wanted to go, too.

"I want to see Samuel," he wailed. "There isn't anyone around here for me to play with."

"Hush that, now," William said sternly. "With Jack away, Mrs. Stone will have all the work on her shoulders, since I'm not able to do much yet. I was hoping ye could help us out, but I see ye're still too much of a bairn to do a man's work."

Jonathan stayed his tears. "I'm no baby! I'm big enough to see to anything that needs doing."

Ann was suddenly sobered by the realization that her brother would have to do a man's work at an early age here, just as he would have if they had stayed in Ireland. But here, at least, he could work toward being independent, and when the time came, he could leave the Stones' grant and claim land of his own. It was one of their father's dreams for him, and Ann could see that it would come to pass.

The Stones were not much for letter-writing, Hannah said, but after some searching, she found paper that Ann could use. Ann thought a long while before she penned a letter to the Andrews expressing her appreciation for their help, and asking their forgiveness for any pain she had caused. She added that she had not used the gold coins, and she intended to return them to James Andrews as soon as she found a safe means of doing so.

To the Alexanders she described her newly found spiritual peace, without going into the details of what had precipitated it, and thanked Jane Alexander for her valuable counsel. She concluded both letters with detailed directions for reaching Stone's clearing, and added that it seemed likely that they would stay there permanently.

Ann added a prayer of her own to William's that night, that in the days ahead, God's will would be done in all their lives.

The next morning Jack and Ann departed for Shawnee Creek, where he stopped at the blacksmith's to leave a tool that needed repair. As she watched Jack conversing with the man, Ann realized that it had been the blacksmith's comment to the trader Yancey that had begun the chain of events that culminated in her finding her father. She did not mention the incident to the blacksmith, however, and she told Jack only part of the story as they rode on toward the river.

"The man that brought you to the clearing—might you be writing to him, by any chance?"

"John Andrews? No, but one of the letters is to his parents. All of us owe them a great debt. We'd never have found Father without the Andrews' help."

"Are you going to marry John Andrews?" Jack asked.

"No," Ann replied.

"That will be good news for the other bachelors around here," Jack said with a smile. "There are plenty of men who'd like to wed if they could find a girl. That's one reason I want to get things settled with Isabel, before someone else comes along and takes her away from me."

Ann recalled that Isabel had wanted to marry a rich man, but she knew that her friend would be happy with Jack, and she was glad for them both.

"What is the Prentiss's store like?" asked Ann as they drew nearer.

"It's not just a store," Jack explained. "It's part inn, part tavern, part freight depot, and the church where the minister holds services when he makes his rounds. There's a dock behind it, where barges and fishing boats and canoes tie up, and a shed on one side where the cattle and horses are kept. There must be eight or ten cabins in the village already, and more being built. Pretty soon it'll be a regular town."

"How often does the minister come? Mr. Smith said a Reverend Grayson would be in Tolliver Station in a week or so."

"We don't usually know, but he always stays around for a week or so, and when the word gets out, couples come in to be married and sometimes he even has a funeral service for all who have died since his last trip. I figure he ought to be back at least once more before winter comes."

It was almost full dark when Jack and Ann rode up to the store, and candles had already been lit inside. As they entered, Ann was reminded of the Blue Boar in Lancaster. Only this place had shelves filled with all manner of goods, running the length of one wall, and plank tables and benches were set in front of a large hearth.

No fire burned in the large fireplace this evening, however, and Ann could see that food was being prepared in a room at the rear. Although both mother and daughter were enveloped in aprons and crowned with white mobcaps covering their hair, Ann immediately recognized Mrs. Prentiss, and then Isabel. When she saw Ann, Isabel screeched and almost dropped the platter of fried fish she was carrying.

"Look what I brought you," Jack said to Isabel.

"I can't believe it!" Isabel cried, as the girls fell into each other's arms. Hearing the commotion, Mary Prentiss, and then Samuel, crowded around Ann, all talking at once.

"How well ye look!" Mrs. Prentiss exclaimed.

"How is the rest of the family?" Tom Prentiss asked. "Are they with ye?"

"And how came ye to know Jack Stone?" Isabel demanded.

"She'll gladly tell you all, but first might we have a bite of supper?" Jack put in, with a broad smile at Isabel. "It's been a good day's ride we've had, and not even a woman can talk on forever without some nourishment."

"Well, food we have," Mary Prentiss said, "and better than the fare on the *Derry Crown*, I can assure ye. Sit down, lass, and eat. Then we want to hear it all."

Ann's condensed version of what had befallen them since their parting with the Prentisses concluded with the news that she expected her father and Hannah Stone to marry.

"It's God's own miracle," Mary declared, her eyes moist. "I canna tell ye how often we've thought o' ye, and the others we traveled with, and wondered how all were faring."

"We often thought of ye, as well. How did ye come to be in this place, yourselves?" Ann asked. "The last we knew, ye were to go down the Delaware."

"Aye, we did that," Tom Prentiss said, "all the way to the Chesapeake Bay. Then we heard about this post on the Susquehanna that could be bought cheap. It's not much now," he added, looking around as if comparing it to his shop in Ireland, "but it's all ours, free and clear, and with the peltry trade this winter, we should do well."

They sat around the table and talked until the candles began to sputter and go out, and Tom Prentiss declared that they must call it a day. Jack went off to share Samuel's bed, and Isabel and Ann climbed a ladder into an attic, where Isabel slept on a straw mattress.

"It gets stuffy up here when the day's been hot," she said, "but at least we have some privacy. Now tell me about Caleb Craighead."

"I told ye he came to see us in Lancaster," Ann replied. "I don't know where he is now, or whether I'll ever see him again. When ye marry Jack and come to live at Stone's clearing, we'll have more time to talk together."

"What makes ye think that I'm going to marry Jack Stone?" Isabel asked, with a twinkle in her eye. "Have ye forgot that I want a rich husband?"

"No, but I think it's unlikely ye'll find one of those

around here, and in the short time I've known the Stones, I have been impressed by them both. Jack and his mother saved my father's life, and I'm sure he'd make a fine husband."

"Don't ye dare tell him I said so," Isabel said in a whisper, "but I was afraid he wouldn't ask me—we've not had much chance to get to know one another."

"Well, rest assured, he will ask ye," Ann said, hugging Isabel, "and I couldn't be happier for the both of ye."

Ann and Jack set out for Stone's clearing after two days at the Prentisses's post. In that time, Jack had asked for and won Isabel's hand in marriage, and Ann's letters had been put into the hands of a bargeman who promised to see that they would reach Lancaster.

"I will let ye know as soon as the minister arrives," Tom Prentiss assured Jack, and Ann promised to return for the wedding.

"There is much to be done before my cabin is fit to receive Isabel," Jack said, "I want her to find everything she needs when she comes into our home." Once again Ann realized that Isabel was fortunate to be marrying such a considerate man.

"Could we make it a double ceremony, then?" William asked, when Jack shared the news of his and Isabel's upcoming wedding. "I'd be honored if Hannah'd be my wife."

"Well, Mr. McKay," Hannah replied, obviously pleased, "it's a dangerous business to say such a thing before witnesses. You'll have no way to back out of it."

"I'll not take it back, but first ye must say that ye will agree to it."

"And that I can gladly do."

"It looks as if we'll have to get the neighbors back

180

over here and build on to this cabin," Jack declared, surveying it with his eyes. "How about three more rooms—one for Ann, one for Jonathan, and one just for cooking? That ought to take care of everyone."

Yes, Ann thought as she listened, everyone was taken care of—almost. Her prayers were for the patience to await God's good time in revealing His purpose for her life.

As the extra rooms were being added to Hannah Stone's cabin, Ann made bedding for the new bunks, stitching homespun linen together and stuffing it with corn husks and straw, then making pillows with feathers Hannah had saved. When finally they were finished late one morning, Ann tied on her bonnet and walked up the ridge west of the cabin, her copy of *The Pilgrim's Progress* in hand. She had discovered that from the top she could see the surrounding country-side rather well. The Stones' cabins were the only dwellings in sight, and only a small portion of the trail was visible as it crossed an open area to the south. The land was wild, and demanding of those who sought to tame it, but Ann already felt deeply attached to it. How far they had come and how many things had happened in the past few months!

Settled in her favorite spot she opened the book once more and began reading, thoughts of her own spiritual journey suddenly seen in a new light. When Christian fell into the Slough of Despond, he was rescued by Help, who told him that every virtuous man sometimes falls into the mire of doubt. Later, when he had been captured by the giant, Despair, and taken to Doubting Castle, Christian was freed by using the key of Promise, and fled with Hopeful as his companion. Eventually, Christian reached Mount Zion to be greeted by angels.

Like Christian, Ann had set out on a journey full of hazards, and like Christian's, many of her worst fears had never materialized. It was true that she had lost her mother, and nearly her father, but both she and Jonathan were safe; they had not succumbed to fever or been attacked by Indians, after all. She had much to be thankful for, not the least of which was her experience of salvation.

So lost was she in thought that the sun passed its zenith unnoticed and made its way into the west to cast her shadow in front of her. As she looked up from the pages of her book, she realized suddenly that she had missed the noon meal, and her continued absence might cause her father alarm.

As Ann stood, she saw that a horseman wearing a black hat and cloak was approaching rapidly from the south, raising dusty plumes as the horse's hooves churned the dry trail. Just before he was lost from view in a grove of trees, Ann caught sight of a glimmer of white at the man's throat. A white shirt, perhaps, or—her breath caught sharply—a clerical collar. She ran down the hill, heedless of the brambles that caught at her skirt and clawed her ankles. She arrived at the clearing breathless, her bonnet askew, her skirt covered with stick-me-tights and briar snags. Still she ran, down the path into the thicket leading to the trail. The rider must have reached the blaze marks on the trees, Ann thought. In a moment, if he kept on the trail, he would soon be out of sight, and she might never know who it was. Or, he might turn west and come up the path to Stone's clearing. The clatter of hooves grew louder, and Ann stopped, her heart hammering, as the horse and rider came into view on the path. Her head swam and she was nearly fainting as she looked up at the rider. At first his head was down, but when he raised it, she saw that it was Caleb Craighead.

In an instant he reined in his horse, dismounted, and came toward her, and his strong arms encircled her. She began to cry, and he cradled her gently, rocking her tenderly in his arms as if he were soothing a child.

"I feared I would never see ye again," Ann said when she could speak.

"I told ye once that I felt convicted that we would meet again," Caleb said, looking intently into her eyes. "Did ye not believe me?"

"All I could do was hope," Ann said. "How did ye know where to find me? Or did ye happen here by accident?"

"It was no accident." he assured her. "When I left Lancaster, I thought ye loved another man and would be happy with him, and that it was best that I let ye be. But I couldn't forget ye. Two weeks ago I was on my way to preach at Drumore when I met John Andrews, and he told me everything that happened," he said, pulling Ann to him again and holding her tightly. "He said ye had found God's peace, and that ye wanted that for him, as well. We prayed together, and John asked Christ to rule his life."

"I am so glad," Ann murmured. "I have prayed that he would. Oh, Caleb, I was so ashamed of what I did—" she began, but he would not let her continue.

"Hush," he said gently. "Whatever you did, God has forgiven, and ye have never wronged me in any way. The important thing now is that we do God's will."

"Yes," Ann whispered, and felt fresh tears of joy as she cradled her head on his shoulder.

Tenderly Caleb lifted her chin and looked into her eyes. "Will ye marry me and share my work, Ann?"

"Yes, Caleb," she said, smiling. At last she knew the direction her life would take. She was about to start a new journey, one ordained by God and one that she prayed He would lead every step of the way.

ABOUT THE AUTHOR

KAY CORNELIUS has been an English teacher for twenty years and, in addition to writing for Serenade Books, has published articles, essays, and devotions.

Kay earned her B.A. degree from George Peabody College for Teachers and later received her Masters of Education degree from Alabama A. & M. University. She has continued her studies at Auburn University. She enjoys travel and researching folklore and history. She and her husband have two children.

A Letter To Our Readers

Dear Reader:

Pioneering is an exhilarating experience, filled with opportunities for exploring new frontiers. The Zondervan Corporation is proud to be the first major publisher to launch a series of inspirational romances designed to inspire and uplift as well as to provide wholesome entertainment. In order that we might better contribute to your reading enjoyment, we would appreciate your taking a few minutes to respond to the following questions and return to:

> Editor, Serenade Books
> The Zondervan Publishing House
> 1415 Lake Drive, S.E.
> Grand Rapids, Michigan   49506

1. Did you enjoy reading LOVE'S GENTLE JOURNEY?

   ☐ Very much. I would like to see more books by this author!
   ☐ Moderately
   ☐ I would have enjoyed it more if _____

2. Where did you purchase this book? _____

3. What influenced your decision to purchase this book?

   ☐ Cover   ☐ Back cover copy
   ☐ Title   ☐ Friends
   ☐ Publicity   ☐ Other _____

4. Please rate the following elements from 1 (poor) to 10 (superior).

☐ Heroine   ☐ Plot
☐ Hero   ☐ Inspirational theme
☐ Setting   ☐ Secondary characters

5. Which settings would you like to see in future Serenade/Saga Books?

_____ _____

_____ _____

6. What are some inspirational themes you would like to see treated in future books?

_____ _____

_____ _____

7. Would you be interested in reading other Serenade/Serenata or Serenade/Saga Books?

☐ Very interested
☐ Moderately interested
☐ Not interested

8. Please indicate your age range:

☐ Under 18   ☐ 25–34   ☐ 46–55
☐ 18–24   ☐ 35–45   ☐ Over 55

9. Would you be interested in a Serenade book club? If so, please give us your name and address:

Name _____

Occupation _____

Address _____

City _____ State _____ Zip _____

Serenade Serenata Books are inspirational romances in contemporary settings, designed to bring you a joyful, heart-lifting reading experience.

Serenade Serenata books available in your local bookstore:

Serenade Saga Books are inspirational romances in historical settings, designed to bring you a joyful, heart-lifting reading experience.

Serenade Saga books available in your local bookstore:

#1 SUMMER SNOW, Sandy Dengler
#2 CALL HER BLESSED, Jeanette Gilge
#3 INA, Karen Baker Kletzing
#4 JULIANA OF CLOVER HILL,
     Brenda Knight Graham
#5 SONG OF THE NEREIDS, Sandy Dengler
#6 ANNA'S ROCKING CHAIR, Elaine Watson
#7 IN LOVE'S OWN TIME,
     Susan C. Feldhake
#8 YANKEE BRIDE, Jane Peart
#9 LIGHT OF MY HEART,
     Kathleen Karr
#10 LOVE BEYOND SURRENDER,
     Susan C. Feldhake
#11 ALL THE DAYS AFTER SUNDAY,
     Jeanette Gilge
#12 WINTERSPRING, Sandy Dengler
#13 HAND ME DOWN THE DAWN,
     Mary Harwell Sayler
#14 REBEL BRIDE, Jane Peart
#15 SPEAK SOFTLY, LOVE, Kathleen Yapp
#16 FROM THIS DAY FORWARD, Kathleen Karr
#17 THE RIVER BETWEEN, Jacquelyn Cook
#18 VALIANT BRIDE, Jane Peart
#19 WAIT FOR THE SUN, Maryn Langer
#20 KINCAID OF CRIPPLE CREEK,
     Peggy Darty
#21 LOVE'S GENTLE JOURNEY,
     Kay Cornelius